THE TREACHEROUS HEART

Titles from Cynthia Harrod-Eagles
by Severn House

Novels

ON WINGS OF LOVE
EVEN CHANCE
LAST RUN
PLAY FOR LOVE
A CORNISH AFFAIR
NOBODY'S FOOL
DANGEROUS LOVE
REAL LIFE (Short Stories)
KEEPING SECRETS
THE LONGEST DANCE
THE HORSEMASTERS
JULIA
THE COLONEL'S DAUGHTER
HARTE'S DESIRE
COUNTRY PLOT
KATE'S PROGRESS
THE HOSTAGE HEART

The Bill Slider Mysteries

GAME OVER
FELL PURPOSE
BODY LINE
KILL MY DARLING
BLOOD NEVER DIES
HARD GOING
STAR FALL
ONE UNDER
OLD BONES
SHADOW PLAY

THE
TREACHEROUS
HEART
Cynthia Harrod-Eagles

Severn House Large Print
London & New York

This first large print edition published 2020
in Great Britain and the USA by
SEVERN HOUSE PUBLISHERS LTD of
Eardley House, 4 Uxbridge Street, London W8 7SY.
First world regular print edition published 2018 by
Severn House Publishers Ltd.

British Library Cataloguing in Publication Data
A CIP catalogue record for this title is available from the British Library.

ISBN-13: 9780727892409

Severn House Publishers support the Forest Stewardship Council™
[FSC™], the leading international forest certification organisation. All
our titles that are printed on FSC certified paper carry the FSC logo.

MIX
Paper from
responsible sources
FSC
www.fsc.org FSC® C013056

Typeset by Palimpsest Book Production Ltd.,
Falkirk, Stirlingshire, Scotland.
Printed and bound in Great Britain by
T J International, Padstow, Cornwall.

One

'Eight o'clock, Anne, love. Time to get up. I've brought you a cup of tea.'

Anne struggled upwards through the mists of sleep at the sound of her father's voice, and with an effort raised herself onto her elbow to take the cup and saucer from her father's hand.

'Thanks, Dad. You shouldn't bother, you know,' she said sleepily. She didn't really like tea in bed first thing in the morning, especially not such a huge cup of strong, dark-brown tea, but Dad did it to be kind, and she couldn't hurt his feelings.

'Oh, it's no trouble, love. Have to keep the workers happy, you know!' He smiled as he said it, but Anne knew that underneath his cheerfulness he didn't really like her to go out to work. His ideas were so old-fashioned that he thought young ladies should stay at home and wait to get married. Anne smiled as her father took himself off to let her get up in privacy. Those days were long gone – if they ever existed! Nowadays, a girl expected to have to work, and happiness came from accepting that, and making the work as interesting as possible. If you took an interest in everything you did, Anne found, the days passed quickly and happily.

However, there wasn't time today to philosophise: it was Thursday, and Thursday was market day in the town of Market Winton where she

1

and her father lived. Anne listened for a moment to make sure where her father was, and then opened the window of her room and poured the tea carefully into the flowerbed outside. Dad had only taken to bringing her tea in the mornings since Mother died, almost a year ago. Anne thought he did it partly because he was lonely for Mum and wanted to fuss over someone, and partly because he thought Anne was lonely. She did miss her mother, of course, but Mum had been ill for a long time, and her death had been what the doctors call a merciful release.

Anne looked out of the window to see what sort of a day it was going to be. It wasn't much of a view from any of the windows – the back side of Winton Parva Station, a piece of waste ground deep with nettles, rose-bay willow herb, yarrow and rusting cars, and the tiny strip of 'garden' Dad had planted between the low wooden fence and the house. He managed to get an amazing amount out of that tiny strip, she thought. He had a passion for the old-fashioned flowers – wallflowers, pansies, stocks and the like – and in among the beds of bright, rich colour, he also grew some vegetables, surprisingly successfully.

Mind you, he did have plenty of time to potter about between trains. Dad was the station-master of Winton Parva, and the fact that he was the sole member of staff showed how little traffic there was on the line now. The job was, in fact, a kind of semi-retirement for him, and he had been given it after losing a foot in an accident on the lines some years ago. Dad was very philosophical about his disability, and always

2

attempted to make light of it. He even joked about the accident itself, referring to it as the day the Waterloo train 'caught him on the hop'.

'Your mother was never happy with the move down here,' Dad had told Anne once. 'She looked on it as coming down in the world. But, you know, though I never let on to her, I think I like it better here. It's peaceful, and I've got my bit of garden, and my bike to take little trips out. I don't think I'd want to move away now.'

The sound of the 8.09 down train jerked Anne from her reverie, and she hastened to wash and dress and get out to the kitchen. Dad always started breakfast before the 8.09; Anne finished the preparations and they ate together before the 8.35 up train called him away again and gave Anne her signal to set off for work. Dad arrived promptly and shrugged off his uniform jacket and hung it on the back of the door before sitting down at the narrow table.

'Breakfast ready, is it, love?'

'Just coming. Many on the train?'

'Quite a lot. Some holidaymakers with tents and a bunch of soldiers. And a crate of pigeons for Tom Jenkins. Could never see any sense in pigeons, myself, unless you eat 'em. Can't pet 'em or play with 'em. Take 'em a hundred miles in a box on a train, let 'em out, and go home again. Where's the fun in that?'

'Not much fun for the pigeons, either, I shouldn't think,' Anne said, bringing the two plates to the table. They ate in silence for a while, and Anne watched her father covertly, knowing what was coming next.

'Rabbits, now, I'll give you rabbits. Nice, pretty, friendly creatures, no smell to speak of, and a lot of nice eating on a rabbit. Rabbits I can understand – but pigeons!'

'You haven't the room for rabbits,' Anne said, as she always did when her father brought up the subject. He had always wanted to keep rabbits, but her mother had had such an aversion to them that he had never done more than talk wistfully about the idea. Now that mother was gone, he reverted to the subject more and more often, but what Anne said was true – there was no room.

'There's all that waste-land. That's a terrible waste of good land, cars and junk and weeds. I could clear a little bit of that and . . .'

'You couldn't. It'd be trespassing,' Anne said firmly.

'It's Railway land,' her father said simply.

'Yes, but it isn't attached to the house. It'd be trespassing. You know how tough the Railways Board was when Romilly Jones dug up that patch and grew cabbages on it.'

Her father sighed and reached for his cup.

'I suppose you're right. But I'd like a few rabbits. Keep me out of mischief between trains.' His eyes gleamed. 'But I suppose you'd know all about trespass and so on. I ought to take your word.'

The Romilly Jones business was one of the few court cases which had been handled by the firm of solicitors for whom Anne worked. They dealt mainly with land and conveyancing and other documentation, but they had taken on the case partly because of Anne's interest, and partly because there had been some thought of contesting ownership of the land in question. But Romilly Jones, a local layabout reputed to be part gypsy, had bitten off more than he could chew in taking on British Rail, and had been soundly beaten. Anne found it a useful check on her father, who tended to look upon everything to do with the railways as belonging to him.

'Well,' said her father at last, pushing his chair back, 'I'd better get across for the train. Leave the washing-up, love, and I'll do it later.'

'O.K., Dad,' Anne said. 'I'll see you later then.'

'Yes, of course, market day today. Well, bring Joe back for tea if he's time,' Dad said, pausing at the door to add wickedly, 'there's a man who'd understand rabbits!'

And he was gone, leaving Anne laughing. Ten minutes later she was on her way herself, cycling the mile and a half into the centre of Market Winton to the office in Church Street of Messrs. Wilson and Paul, Solicitors and Commissioners for Oaths. The ten minutes were spent putting on her careful makeup and attending to her hair. In the wake of seeing the film of *The Great Gatsby*, Anne had had her hair restyled in the fashion of the thirties, shorter at the back, jaw-length at the front, and very smooth and straight, which made the most of its dark brown thickness and its copper lights. It suited her rather piquant features, her high cheekbones, large eyes, and small, full mouth, and she complemented the hairstyle with the makeup of the same period.

It took care to achieve the right effect, and

5

since it couldn't be hurried, she always set aside enough time in the morning for the task. Anne was not by nature a methodical girl, but when she had applied for the job as secretary to the firm, she had been taken on on a six weeks' trial basis, because the head of the firm, Mr Cass, had thought her too young and probably too flighty for the position. For six weeks she had kept up a mind-boggling effort to appear mature, steady, efficient, methodical and reliable . . . all the things she was not.

The effort had been worth it, for she had been confirmed in the position, and now, four years later, she was still there, and much valued by both partners. The sustained pretence had by now become such second nature to her that she almost was all those things they thought her to be, and since she strove to make her job interesting by getting absorbed in the business the firm transacted, she was also becoming quite knowledgeable in legal matters, which added to her air of staid respectability.

Her natural sense of fun had to be kept for her time off, for evenings and weekends, and it was that side of her which made her so look forward to Thursdays – market day. At ten to nine the town was already busy, with cars pulling trailers making their slow way through the narrow streets to the market ground, and cattle-lorries scraping another layer of stone off the corner of the public house which jutted out at the junction of Cow Lane and Market Street. The town of Market Winton had never been designed for motor traffic, and later in the day it would be full of cursing motorists losing themselves in the temporary one-way systems.

Anne herself had had experience of these one-way systems, and her private opinion was that they had been designed by the police as a punishment for those drivers who were perverse enough to bring their cars into the town centre on a Thursday. Once in the system it was impossible to get out again, for whatever turnings you took, you always ended up in the Town Square, half a mile from the market. Eventually, you yielded to the inevitable, parked the car alongside the horse-trough, and walked the rest of the way.

Church Street was within sight of the market place, and Anne felt the first tremors of excitement at the noise and bustle that was already building up. She wheeled her bicycle across the road and parked it in the bike-rack behind the new Commercial Union building which was next door to the old grey stone house, on the upper floor of which was her office. She drew the enormous heavy key out of her handbag, unlocked the door, and with a last glance at the market place, went in.

That she had the key to the office was a sign of the firm's confidence in her. Mr Whetlore, the younger partner, who lived four miles away at Winton Magna, had the other key. Mr Cass, the senior partner, drove in each day from his large house at Blandford, and relied on one or the other of them to be there first. Mr Cass never came in before 10.30, feeling that at his time of life that was a civilised hour to think of starting work, but Mr Whetlore was keen and also liked to surprise Anne – keep her on her toes, as he put it – and was occasionally in before her.

He arrived this morning on the dot of nine, and appeared rather disappointed not to have pipped Anne to the post.

'Ah, good morning Miss Symons. On time this morning I see.'

Anne, with a straight face, pretended to misunderstand him. 'Good morning, Mr Whetlore, yes, you are on time. I was a little early today.'

'Hmph,' he said. 'Well, bring the post in straight away, will you?' and he disappeared into his office, rather crestfallen. Anne smiled to herself. Round one to me, she thought. Mr Whetlore was the son of the man who had bought out the business from the original partners, Wilson and Paul, and for that reason Mr Cass still sometimes referred to him as 'young Mr Whetlore.' Mr Cass was about sixty-eight, so perhaps Mr Whetlore appeared young to him, but since the younger partner was nearing fifty, the title always amused Anne.

Anne opened and sorted the mail, taking note of one or two matters in which she was taking a particular interest, and then she took the pile of letters in to Mr Whetlore and stood beside the desk while he went through them and took a private look at Anne's appearance. It was for this 'morning inspection' as she called it that Anne took the trouble with her appearance. Mr Whetlore was not above commenting on anything he found wrong. He had a secret dislike of women in offices, and was glad to find fault if he could. At first it had terrified Anne, for it was her first job, and she didn't know whether she might be dismissed out of hand if anything were amiss.

Now, four years later, she found the situation amusing, and with all the confidence she had built up over those years she looked upon the inspection as a kind of a game: as she grew more difficult to fault, Mr Whetlore's standards became more exacting, and the more he tried to catch her out, the more delighted she was to ape the perfect secretary and disappoint him. It was another of the ways in which she enlivened her life, which otherwise might fall into the trap of routine and become dull.

For routine was one of the things Anne dreaded, even though, inevitably, most of her life was ruled by it. In her secret heart she believed life ought to be exciting and surprising, and she believed that she was the sort of girl who could cope with excitement and danger. One of her favourite pastimes was reading – she went through two books a week from the library, as well as her magazines – and whenever she read, she plunged right into the world in the book, becoming the heroine, or even hero, in her own mind until dear, sleepy old Winton and the solicitor's office were far away and forgotten.

Of course, it was very unlikely that anything remotely exciting would ever happen to her, living and working as she did in a small country town, where the one high spot was the weekly market. But she had inherited from her father a strong streak of the ability to 'make do.' He had always wanted a garden, but had to make do

9

with a strip ten feet by three. Into that strip, however, he crammed more than most gardeners got into their whole garden, and she was sure he had more pleasure out of that strip than the owner of a hundred and fifty feet could possibly have. In the same way Anne built up the weekly market in her own mind and extracted every last ounce from it.

The market was not the only source of entertainment, of course. Like all towns, Winton had its cinemas, pubs and discos, along with various more rural entertainments. Anne enjoyed them all. She liked the jumble sales and whist drives and school concerts and gymkhanas and flower shows. She went to the open day at the army camp and the NAAFI dances and even helped with the old folks' tea party held in the town hall each December. If adventure was going to seek Anne out, it would have no difficulty in finding her, that was sure.

At half past ten, while Anne was doing some filing, Mr Cass arrived.

'Good morning, Miss Symons. What a lovely day! I always think it's especially nice when our good weather falls on a Thursday,' he greeted her.

'Yes, isn't it lovely,' she replied, smiling. She liked Mr Cass, having a private idea that he was really rather wicked, and had a sense of humour which he indulged at young Mr Whetlore's expense. Mr Cass hung up his hat and coat carefully and brushed them with the flat of his hand. He had bought them when he was first made a senior partner of the firm, and didn't intend ever to replace them. Then he started on the long trek to his office, on the other side of the room. He moved so slowly Anne sometimes wondered if he'd make it before lunch.

As he reached the door of his room, he turned and said to Anne, as he did every morning,

'Ah, Miss Symons, I wonder if you could possibly rustle up a cup of coffee for me?'

It was part of Anne's duties to make coffee in the morning and tea in the afternoon for both partners, but Mr Cass always made it sound like a favour, which was one of the reasons she liked him.

'Certainly, Mr Cass. I'll put the kettle on now.'

'Thank you, Miss Symons. And then you can go for your own coffee, of course. I hear tell,' and his eyes twinkled gravely, 'they have doughnuts at the Cosy Café this morning.'

'Would you like me to bring you one back?' Anne asked innocently. Mr Cass pretended to look offended.

'I mentioned it only out of academic interest, Miss Symons.'

On Thursdays, after she had made the partners their coffee, Anne always went out to the Cosy Café at the corner of Church Street for her own coffee break. It was one of the little treats that made Thursdays special. She never really knew whether Mr Cass was hinting or not when he said things like that. Sometimes she brought him back a cake to have with his tea, and sometimes he accepted it, and sometimes he didn't. It all added to the variety.

At five to eleven, Anne switched off her

typewriter, picked up her handbag and crossed the street to the café. It was one of those arty little places with fumed oak tables, and windsor chairs with chinz seat-cushions, but the oak beams that ran across the low ceiling were genuine enough, and the coffee was good. Anne usually met her friend from school days, Wendy Stokes, for coffee here on Thursdays, and Wendy was already there, sitting at a table and watching the door.

'Ah, there you are. I didn't get my coffee – I thought I'd wait for you," Wendy said as she came in.

'You're early, aren't you?'

'Dear old punctual Anne! I don't know, I believe you sit up there at your window with a stop watch waiting to see me come down the street.'

'Don't be silly, it's just that you gave the impression of having been sitting there for some time. Shall we go and order?'

The two girls went down to the counter together. Wendy also worked for solicitors, but hers was quite a different kind of firm from Wilson and Paul. It was a new firm of four young men and occupied offices in the brand new building beside the car park at the back of Woolworth's. It did a lot of business, and had a name for being bright, go-ahead and up to all the modern trends. Mr Whetlore spoke of the partners disparagingly as 'thrusters' and hinted that none of them knew the first thing about the law. Mr Cass said more mildly that there was room in the world for all sorts of firms but that

12

nothing would ever replace the old family lawyer – the 'man of business'.

Wendy liked her job, and spoke rather patronisingly of Anne's, even though she was only one of three typists in the office, and hadn't the sole responsibility that Anne had. She was a plump, pretty girl with vivid blue eyes, and was as perpetually untidy and disorganised as Anne was neat and punctual.

'Two coffees, please,' Wendy said to the girl behind the counter, and then turned her eyes to the display of cakes in the glass-fronted counter. 'Look at those scrummy doughnuts.'

'I thought you were on a diet.' Anne commented mildly.

'I am. I was only saying look at them,' Wendy said indignantly. They did look good – the Cosy Café was noted for its cakes, all home-baked. Both girls usually had something with their coffee as part of the Thursday morning treat, but Wendy sometimes had pangs of conscience about it. She was almost always on a diet, but since she almost always cheated, it cancelled itself out and she stayed the same shape, which was the shape nature intended her to be, and which, in Anne's opinion, suited her very well.

'I think I'll have a rum baba,' Anne said, looking up at the assistant, who nodded.

'You'll have what? Well, what a greedy pig,' Wendy said. 'In that case, I'll have something too. I was going to go without, but since you're setting me such a bad example, let me see.' She mused over the glass case while Anne watched her with amusement.

13

'You know perfectly well,' she said at last, 'that you always have the same as me, so why pretend to choose?'

'That's half the fun, choosing,' Wendy said with a grin. 'All right, I'll be different today – I'll have a rum baba.'

The assistant, looking thoroughly bewildered, served her, and they took their coffee and made their way back to their favourite seat by the window.

'Well now,' Wendy said when they were settled. 'What's the news? What have you been doing since this time last week? What exciting adventures have come your way. Tell Aunty Wendy all, don't spare the details.'

'That won't take long,' Anne said, smiling. 'I went to the disco on Saturday night, which you know because you were there. I went blackberrying with Dad on Sunday, and to the pictures on Sunday night, and the rest of the week has been work. Now you tell – what have you been doing? Are you still going out with Graham?'

'I'm not sure,' Wendy said.

'How can you not be sure? You seemed friendly enough with him on Saturday night.'

Graham Raphael was one of the young accountants who shared the office building with Wendy's firm of solicitors, and the big excitement of last week had been his asking Wendy out. Wendy had hailed it as The Big Romance, but since she started one of those about once a month, Anne had not taken it too seriously.

'Yes, I know, but we had a quarrel on the way home, and then we had a sort of disagreement on Sunday, so I don't think we're speaking to each other at the moment," Wendy said.

'I see,' Anne said. 'I'm finding it increasingly difficult to keep up with your romances – they seem to be on and off more quickly than ever. Aren't you ever afraid you'll run out of new men?'

'Of course not,' Wendy said airily. 'There are plenty of fish in the sea, even in a one-horse town like Winton. And I get bored with the poor fellas so easily. Why don't you try your hand, Anne? You might find you enjoy it. I'm sure you can't have much fun going about with poor old Joe. After all, you've been going out with him for – well, ever since we left school, and that must be four years now.'

'I know,' Anne said, not without a sigh. 'It is a long time. But I like Joe, and he's very fond of me, you know.'

'I know,' Wendy said impatiently. 'And you don't like to hurt his feelings. But you know perfectly well he doesn't appreciate you. All he really loves is pigs, and you're the wrong shape to compete with them.'

Anne laughed. 'You're absurd,' she said, and to turn the conversation away from herself, she asked, 'So if it isn't Graham, who is it?'

'Well, I'm temporarily out of boyfriends at this moment in time,' she said solemnly, 'so if anyone comes along who's extremely handsome, fairly rich, young, amusing, a man of the world, has good taste—'

Her voice trailed off and both girls stared in the same direction. Through the big, plate-glass window of the café they had a fine view of the street, and as Wendy was speaking the very person she had been describing was walking towards them on the opposite side of the street. He was tall, handsome, elegant, dressed in the kind of clothes that you couldn't get on the never-never at a chain-tailors in Winton High Street. He had an air of sophistication that spoke of larger fish-ponds than Market Winton, and as he came closer, Anne found herself gazing at his face and realising that as well as being handsome, it was attractive – not always the same thing.

He seemed to be strolling without great purpose, and when he saw the café he crossed the street and came in, and went through to the counter at the back without a glance at the two girls. They had both hastily withdrawn their eyes as he came in, not wanting to be caught staring at him, but when he had gone past, Wendy took another quick look and then said to Anne in an undertone,

'Wheee! *Who* is that, I wonder?'

'I don't know. I've never seen him before.'

'It must be meant for me. Just when I'm short of an escort – and on market day too. He's like something in a Martini advert. Now,' she leaned across the table with a mock serious air, 'before I crash in and help myself, are you sure you wouldn't like to have first go? Just for a change?'

Anne laughed. 'You are terrible! It's a good job I know you're only joking. Anyway, he wouldn't look at me, or you. Too sophisticated by half.' She refused to turn her head and look

16

at him again. They were both too old for that kind of thing. 'Anyway, don't get yourself excited – he's probably only passing through.'

Wendy sighed. 'Don't I know it. Things like that don't happen in real life. Never mind, Graham's really quite as good looking as that, and probably lots nicer.'

'So Graham's "on" again, is he?'

'He will be by this afternoon,' Wendy said cheerfully. 'We'd better be getting back, you know, it's a quarter past already. Listen, I'll see you at the market this afternoon. See if you can coax Joe away from his pigs to take you into the fair – I want to show off how good Graham is on the rifle range.'

'I'll try, but I doubt if he'll come,' Anne said.

'Tell him there's bowling for a pig,' Wendy directed wisely. 'That'll fetch him.'

'Don't mock,' Anne said, but she laughed all the same. Wendy was not far wrong.

Two

Anne had known Joe Halderthay for a very long time. He had gone to the same secondary school as she had, but being a few years older than her, he had not noticed her. Anne, however, had noticed Joe, and from early days he had been a sort of hero to her.

He was the school sports champion – football, cricket, athletics, swimming – and all-round sportsman, and, as such people will be, very popular with both boys and girls in the school. He was not particularly good at his lessons, but he was good-natured and honest, and these things shone through even to little girls in the lower school. Besides, he was considered very good looking – not especially tall, but broad-shouldered and athletic, fair-skinned, auburnhaired, blue-eyed – a real Dorsetman. By the time he left school and was beginning to take an interest in girls, Anne was not the only one who hung about the gates after school to get a glimpse of him passing on his bike, or lined the playing-field during matches to cheer him.

Joe left school and went to work on a farm over towards Felsham, about five miles from Winton Parva where Anne lived. Farm hands work long hours, and Joe scarcely ever visited the haunts of young people. It was known that he was going out with one of the daughters of the farm manager, and in the fullness of time, never seeing him, Anne forgot him, and had she been asked would have assumed he had married the girl. So that should have been that.

Anne, too, left school and did a secretarial course at the technical college in Weymouth – a great adventure that, travelling in by train every day like a commuter. She had a lot of fun during that year, mixing with boys and girls her own age, having money in her pocket for the first time and no responsibilities, and all the diversions of Weymouth at her command. She found that she was popular with the boys, and was never short of a companion, and from the same source she discovered that she was pretty, so life was fine by her.

She was lucky, too, in spotting the advertisement for the solicitors job when she did and in making a good enough impression at her interview to be taken on. For some time after that she was fully occupied with her job and the necessity of making a good impression. She didn't go out much, spending her evenings repairing and improvising clothes, and going to bed early so as to be sure of getting in on time the next day, and so one by one she lost contact with her old friends.

Her mother was ill at that time, too, so there wasn't the impetus to go out. Her mother had often tried to persuade her, and her father had even been worried because she wasn't bringing young men home for him to interview.

'If you're not careful, my girl,' he had said, 'you'll be too late. You'll wake up one morning and find yourself on the shelf.'

19

'Don't be silly, Dad,' Anne had said. It was too early to worry about *that* sort of thing.

What did happen, however, was that one morning she woke up and found herself bored, and that was the day that Fate took a hand. She was opening the second post at around eleven that morning, when the street door opened and in came a tall, suntanned figure.

'Good morning,' he said, in such a low voice that it failed altogether, and he had to cough and start again. 'Good morning. I wondered if I could see the solicitor?'

He was evidently a farmer, by his shapeless tweed jacket and his clean white shirt, and he was evidently painfully shy. Anne smiled her kindest smile and said, 'I should think so. Can you tell me what's it's about?'

'Well, you see,' he began, and at that moment lifted his eyes for the first time and looked at her. Two things happend. Firstly, he became tongue-tied again and stopped in mid sentence. Secondly, Anne recognised her former hero of the sports field.

'Why, you're Joe Halderthay, aren't you?' she cried. He looked surprised and confused.

'Well, yes, I am, but I'm afraid . . .?'

'Oh, I don't suppose you'd remember me. Anne Symons. I was a few years younger than you.'

'Yes, I do – I do remember you, of course,' he said and as Anne raised an eyebrow, thinking he was simply being polite, he went on, 'you lived in Winton Parva, by the railway station.'

'I still do,' Anne said, impressed by his memory.

'Fancy you remembering that. I never supposed you even noticed me.'

'Oh yes,' he said eagerly, 'I always thought you were—' He broke off, looking confused, and though Anne prompted him gently he wouldn't go on.

'So what are you doing these days?' she asked in the end.

'I'm a stockman on Haldane's Farm,' he said.

'Cattle?' Anne asked.

'Pigs,' he replied, and a gleam of pleasure lit his eyes at the very word. 'I'm specialising in them, especially in the breeding. Fascinating animals.'

'I don't know that I've ever cared for them,' Anne said, wrinkling her nose, 'though I suppose they're better than sheep. What does your wife think?'

'I'm sorry?'

'Of the pigs? Does she like pigs?'

'My wife? But I'm not married,' he said, bewildered.

'Oh dear, I'm sorry. I thought you were married to – what's her name? – the eldest Moore girl. You used to work on their farm, didn't you?'

'That was Jenny. Yes, I used to go out with her when I worked at Moore's, but we broke it off when I went to Haldane's. We were never serious about each other anyway.'

'I always assumed you married her, I don't know why,' Anne said vaguely.

'I think she married a chap from the Atomic factory in the end, 'Joe said. 'And what about you? What do you do?'

'Well, as you see,' Anne said, waving a hand round the office. 'I work here.'

Joe was abashed again. 'Of course, silly of me,' he muttered. He was silent, and Anne realised that she still didn't know what he had come for. She waited for him to say something, and since it appeared that he was tongue-tied again, she prompted him gently,

'You were going to tell me what you came to see us about, when I interrupted you.'

'Oh yes, well you see, I'm hoping in the end to buy a place of my own and set up in pigs. I'm head stockman now on Haldane's and I'm studying at night, and I should be able to get a manager's job in a year or two. Then I'll be able to save up to get a deposit on a place.' He forgot his shyness when he was talking about his favourite subject, and Anne noticed how handsome he looked when his eyes shone and his expression was animated. 'There are special arrangements for mortgages on farm-land, special rates and so on, and with a couple of years as a manager behind me, and a cash deposit, I think I could get a mortgage on a smallish place, enough to set up for a start.'

'How would you buy the stock?' Anne asked.

'That's covered by the mortgage too,' Joe said, evidently pleased that she was taking an interest in his plans. 'I've even seen a bit of land that I think would be just the thing. It's lying fallow at the moment, and there's a cottage on the land, falling down, and hardly any roof on it. It looks as though it's been empty for years.'

'Where is it?' Anne asked. Anything to do with land interested her.

22

'It's out on the Weymouth road, about three or four miles out of Springbourne.'

'I think I know where you mean,' Anne said. 'There's a little side turning, just the other side of that big Dutch barn, then it all lies uphill.'

'That's right, you've got it. Well-drained land. And that's why I came here. I thought you might be able to tell me who owns it, and why it's not being farmed. I suppose it's early days yet to be enquiring about land, when I haven't even got my manager's job yet, but it's on my mind so much I thought I'd have to find out.'

'Well I'm sure we can help you,' Anne said, and then, 'just out of interest, why did you choose this particular firm? Rather than any other?'

'I don't know. I saw the sign in the window, you see – you can see this window from the market. I'm up here every Thursday for the market. I asked one or two people, and they said this was an old-fashioned kind of family firm, so I thought you'd be more likely to know about that sort of thing. Why do you ask?'

'Oh, no reason, really, just interested,' Anne said.

'You seem to be interested in a lot of things,' Joe said, for him greatly daring. Anne smiled.

'You hold on here for a minute, Joe, and I'll see if Mr Cass will see you now, to save you coming back again. I'm sure it must be hard for you to get time off from the farm.'

She left him there and slipped into Mr Cass's office. She couldn't let poor Joe be eaten alive by Mr Whetlore. And in any case, Mr Cass knew practically every inch of this part of Dorset, having done the conveyancing on nearly every part that had ever changed hands.

Anne explained to her boss what was wanted, and Mr Cass agreed to see Joe.

'If it's a friend of yours, Anne, I think it's the least I can do,' he said, unbending for the first time since she had joined the company. She thanked him, and went back to the outer office.

'If you'd like to come through, Joe, Mr Cass will see you now.'

Joe jumped up nervously, and she showed him in. If he had been a cap-wearer, he would have been twisting it in his hands. Anne shut the door after him, and went smiling back to her desk.

She had expected their interview to last only a few moments, but as the time passed and Joe didn't come out, Anne got on with her work and had quite forgotten he was in there by the time the inner door opened again.

'Well, goodbye, and thanks very much,' Joe was saying, and he came out and shut the door.

'Everything O.K.?' Anne asked him.

'Oh, yes, thanks. He's very nice isn't he?'

'Mr Cass? Yes, I think so. Did he tell you what you wanted to know?'

'He thinks the land belongs to a trust set up for a minor, but he's going to find out for sure and let me know. He says if that's the case, the land could be sold when the minor comes of age, which would probably be in a few years' time. That would suit me just fine.'

'So it would,' Anne said. 'Well, I'm very pleased for you.'

She looked up at him patiently. He was standing

on the other side of her desk and she was waiting for him to take his departure before she went on with her work, but he didn't seem in any hurry to go. She wondered suddenly if he thought he had to pay her for the interview, and to help him out, she said,

'Mr Cass will send you his bill when he's finished doing what you asked. I don't expect it will be too much.' She would have the handling of the correspondence, of course, so she could keep an eye on that aspect of things.

'Yes, I see,' Joe said. There was another silence, at the end of which both of them spoke at once.

'Do you—'

'I hope—'

'Go on,' Joe said.

'I was just going to say I hope everything goes all right for you. What were you going to say?'

'Do you like working here,' Joe said after a measurable pause, and Anne had the feeling that was not what he'd meant to say at all.

'Oh yes, I find it very interesting. It has its dull moments, like any job, of course, but that can't be helped. And it's nice working right in town like this.'

'I suppose you go out a lot, in the evenings, I mean?' Joe said next.

'Not a lot,' Anne said. 'My mother's not well, and I tend to stay home to keep her company.'

'Oh,' he said, and seemed disappointed. Anne now had an inkling of what he was aiming at, and she waited, amused, to see how long he took to get there.

'But you go out at the weekends? I suppose you have lots of – friends.'

'I do go out, when I've someone to go with. I seem to have lost touch with most of my friends from the old days, so I don't seem to get asked very much.'

'I wondered,' Joe began, looking in any direction but at her.

'Yes?'

'I wondered if . . . if you would think of . . . perhaps . . . if I could take you out somewhere?' He got it out at last. His face was red under the tan, but Anne had no inclination to laugh at him. He was not ridiculous, only rather endearing.

'Yes, I think I'd like that, Joe. When had you in mind?'

'Well, I don't know if it's possible for you, but I was thinking of maybe Thursday, after the market. I'm in town anyway, you see, and I could get a wash and change at the hotel and then pick you up by about seven. It isn't easy to get away other days, not until quite late.'

'Well, Thursday would be fine by me. You'll come and pick me up, you say?'

'Yes, you still live in the same place, don't you?'

'Yes, by the station. All right, Thursday at about seven, then?'

'I won't be late,' he promised. He smiled at her now, and seemed about to say something else, but closed his mouth again and simply nodded, smiled, and left.

She broke the good news to her father when she got home that night.

'Someone's coming to pick me up and take me out on Thursday, Dad,' she said as she sat down to her tea.

'A young man?' he asked eagerly.

'Is it someone we know, dear?' her mother asked.

'I don't know if you know him. He was at the same school as me, but he's older – we weren't in the same class.'

'Well, what's he called?' Dad asked.

'Joe Halderthay.'

'I don't know the name.'

'He was very good at sports, won all the cups on sports day,' Anne said.

'Oh, that big red-headed boy?' her mother said. 'I remember him, though I didn't know his name.'

'And what does he do for a living?' Dad asked sternly. Anne began to laugh.

'Now, Dad, you mustn't put him through the Spanish Inquisition when he comes on Thursday. He's very shy – and in any case, I'm not thinking of marrying him. I'm only going to go out with him for an evening.'

'You never know what may come of it,' her father warned her. 'Anyway, I have to know if he's a suitable person for my girl to go out with.'

'I'm sure he's very suitable, Dad. He's clean and well-mannered and he's a stockman on Haldane's farm. I'm sure if you rang them up they'd give him a reference.'

Her father stared for a moment, and then reached over and pinched her cheek.

'None of your sauce, Miss Anne. All right, so

I fuss a bit, but you're my only daughter, and you'll have one one day and then you'll know how I feel.'

Anne smiled back at him. 'I know how you feel Dad. And Joe Halderthay is respectable enough to suit even you.'

At seven o'clock precisely a knock on the door heralded Joe's arrival, and Dad hurried to the door to get a look at him before Anne could intervene. By the time Anne reached them, they were seated in the sitting room, and Joe was telling Dad about his job at Haldane's. As Anne came in he jumped to his feet, and Anne was pleased with his good manners, not only for herself but for the impression it would have on Dad.

'Hello, Joe. You're punctual,' she said. Joe had made good use of the hotel washroom. He was shaved so close that his face was red even through his tan, and he fairly gleamed with cleanliness. Anne could smell the soap across the room. He had on a clean white shirt and a tie under a check jacket which, though shapeless, was evidently not his working jacket, and wore well-pressed grey flannel trousers. When she reflected that he must have been carrying those trousers round with him all day, she realised that some maid at the hotel must have taken pity on him and ironed them for him.

He had taken so much trouble over his appearance that Anne was touched, and as she came forward, he fumbled in his pocket and brought out a small box of chocolates, which he handed to her.

'I got these for you,' he said hesitantly. She

28

took the box, hardly knowing what to say. The gesture was so old-fashioned, but so thoughtful, that it made her want to cry. She hadn't the least idea of what she was supposed to do with the chocolates – open them and hand them round? – and probably neither had Joe, but he knew that when you went to pick up a girl on your first date you took her a present, so that's what he had done.

Anne's mouth opened and shut again, and she looked helplessly at her father. He nodded and smiled, as if to say, yes, that's quite correct. That's what should be done. He and Joe would get on together, Anne thought.

'Thank you, Joe,' she said 'It's very kind of you. I – I'll just go and get my coat. I won't keep you waiting.'

'Oh, no hurry, please,' Joe said, and she made her escape. When she returned with her coat, he was on his feet again in an instant to help her into it, and she had enough presence of mind to accept his help gracefully.

'We'll be off, then, Dad. I have my key, so you don't need to wait up if I'm late.'

'I'll bring her back in good time, Mr Symons,' Joe said, and Dad smiled complaisantly.

'I know you will, Joe. Have a good time, both of you.'

Outside, Joe fell in beside her and asked.

'Where would you like to go?'

Anne had expected him to have decided, but on reflection realised that it would be for her to be indulged, not him. She thought of the chocolates.

'What about the cinema? Or doesn't that appeal to you?'

'That's all right by me. Do you know what's on?'

'No, but we could find out,' Anne said. Joe nodded, and became masterful.

'We'll drive in and look at both of them, and then you can choose. The car's just along here.'

She understood how it was to be. She would decide what they would do, and he would arrange all the details. Well, it was a pleasant way to divide the duties. They turned the corner of the road, and Anne saw the vehicle with which she was to form an intimate acquaintance. Car was a polite term for it. It was in fact a very old van, with windows of perspex set into the sides at the back. The back door was secured with string. One of the wing mirrors was missing, and where you could see through the mud, the paint was scratched and the rust showed through.

Inside there were bucket seats at the front, and the back was filled with sacks and bales of wire and tools and newspapers and bottles of pig-drench and worming powders and a tarpaulin and some bits of wood and various other items of farm rubble. Anne was only surprised there were no pigs in there, for she could certainly smell them.

'I'm sorry the van's in a bit of a state, but it's the farm van, you see,' Joe said.

'I see,' Anne said dourly.

'But I brought a clean blanket to put over your seat so as to keep your clothes clean,' Joe said, suiting his actions to his words. He had thought of everything, Anne thought, and could only sit herself graciously on the freshly-laundered blanket that was spread for her, and allow herself to be driven away.

They decided to see the film at the Roxy, which was the first cinema they went to. Joe bought the best seats, and they ate her chocolates during the film, and ice-cream during the interval. It was a good film, and Anne enjoyed it, but was painfully aware of Joe beside her all the time. She rather expected her hand to be taken, but he did not make any move towards touching her right through the film, and sitting there expecting it and not having it happen was nerve-racking.

When the film was over it was still quite early, and Joe asked her if she'd like to go somewhere else.

'For a drink, perhaps?' he asked. 'Or if you prefer coffee, there a café along the road here.'

'Which would you prefer, Joe?' Anne asked, but she wasn't going to get away with that.

'It's for you to choose,' he said firmly, and in the end she said she was rather hungry, so they went to a coffee bar and had a hamburger. There were a lot of young people there, and among them Wendy Stokes with her boyfriend of the moment. Wendy spotted Anne and Joe as they came in, and brought her friend over to join them, so another old acquaintance was revived that day, and it was from that meeting that their regular Thursday coffee-morning arose.

In due course Joe decided that it was late enough and told Anne that he was taking her home. He did it very politely, as he did everything, but Anne had the feeling that had she

31

argued with him she would have come off worst. They chatted as they drove back to Winton Parva, but when he pulled up the car at her home he fell suddenly silent. In the quiet and darkness, Anne felt the hair rising with anticipation on the back of her neck, and looking sideways at Joe's profile in the faint starlight, she got the impression he was having an internal battle with himself.

At last he turned to her, and said in a husky voice.

'Anne, it's very good of you to come out with me.'

'Not good at all,' she protested. 'I've enjoyed myself.'

'Have you? I'm so glad. I thought you might be bored. I'm not much of a conversationalist. Well, I've always thought I was a bit dull – but – well, if you haven't been too bored, I mean, if you could possibly—'

'Out with it, Joe,' Anne teased him gently. 'If I could what?'

'Would you come out with me again?' he asked, and his voice held little hope.

'I'd love to,' she said, putting all her enthusiasm into her voice. His eyes met her, surprised and happy. She wondered why she had said it. She had enjoyed herself, but she thought another few evenings like that would leave her bored, and then how would she explain to him? How could she ever break off, once she had started?

There was no moon that night, and the nearest lamp-post was a hundred yards away. The faint starlight was all they had to see by, but it lit the edges of Joe's face, and picked out the crest of hair at the front where the sun had bleached his auburn to blonde. It was cool, and she could feel the warmth of him close by. His lips looked firm and cool, and she wondered what it would be like to be kissed by him. She felt her heart thumping as she waited, and saw again the struggle in his face.

But he didn't. It was their first 'date', and he knew that you didn't kiss a girl the first time out. They shook hands to say goodbye, having made an arrangement to meet on Saturday night, and he drove away. Anne had to wait for some time before he first got round to kissing her and she sometimes thought, in the years that followed, that if he had kissed her that first evening by starlight, she might have fallen in love with him. It might all have been quite different.

Three

On Thursdays Anne's working day finished at two o'clock. By five past two she had covered her typewriter, said goodbye to her bosses, and was out in the street and heading for the market. The uncertain weather of the morning had given way to a sunny afternoon and added to the holiday feeling that never failed her on market day. All the streets round and near the market were lined with parked cars, and from the market place itself came a mixture of sounds and smells that Anne would have recognised anywhere.

On this particular Thursday there was in addition another set of smells and sounds, belonging to the fairground which had been set up on the field next to the market. This field was usually used for parking on Thursdays, and its annexation had caused even more parking problems in the town. Every inch of roadside was being pressed into use, and the two old men who directed the traffic in the market grounds were almost weeping with frustration as they tried to wave cars away from the part of the parking-field which had been reserved for lorries and cattle-trucks.

It will all sort itself out by tomorrow, Anne thought. They had this problem every year, any time anything unusual happened, like summer arriving. It was a problem to be expected in a small town not designed for the age of the internal combustion engine. Mind you, she added to herself, it couldn't have been much fun negotiating those narrow streets even in a horse and cart. It was difficult to imagine any kind of movement for which the town could have been designed. The answer must be that it wasn't designed at all, but just happened . . .

Anne made her way first of all to the cattle market. She was to meet Joe for a snack lunch, but by experience she knew that he would still be embroiled with his Large White weaners, and wouldn't be able to spare her any attention for the moment. The cattle market was her favourite section, and she went first of all to the long shed where the calves were tethered. There was the usual clutch of holidaymakers petting the calves and oohing and aahing over them. The stockmen stood around watching them cynically. It was generally the weakly undersized calves that interested the holidaymakers, and it had been known for a farmer to sell one of these calves at a large profit to some softhearted tripper with more money than sense.

The calves on the whole took their fate calmly, many of them lying folded up on the scanty straw and chewing the cud in a bored way. Not so the young bullocks, who milled around in their pens and bellowed like a colossal, collective belly-ache. There would be the occasional moment of calm, and then another would let out a yell and start them all off again. They threw each other into a panic, and charged round with their heads up, banging into each other with their blunted horns.

Anne passed the pens of dairy cows, and stopped when she came to a high-fenced pen in which stood a large and beautiful bull. He was a white-faced Hereford with curly ginger hair and he flicked his hairy ears in an endearing kind of way and rolled a sad eye at Anne as she paused. A young boy she knew by sight was sitting on the top rail of the pen and slapping his leg with a whittled stick.

'Hullo,' Anne said.

''lo,' he replied. He looked in the opposite direction, elaborately casual.

'He's a nice-looking fellow,' she said politely, referring to the bull. 'Why are they selling him?'

'Got another,' the boy said. The bull sighed heavily and pushed his wet pink nose against the railings in Anne's direction. She pushed a hand through and scratched behind his horns, and he sighed again, more happily.

'There's nothing wrong with him, is there?' she asked.

'No,' said the boy fiercely, looking at her for a moment, and then away again, scarlet-faced. 'Just got another, that's all. Bred two 'n' chose the best.' The bull turned his head a little to let Anne get at the sensitive places more easily. 'I like this'n best,' the boy volunteered. 'T'other'n's bad-tempered.'

'Well, this old boy is certainly friendly,' Anne said, and the boy almost smiled with pleasure at hearing his favourite praised. He suddenly became communicative.

'I seen you out 'th Joe – from up Haldane's. Are you 'n him going to get married?'

Now it was Anne's turn to be embarrassed. 'I don't know,' she said. 'I hadn't thought about it.'

'Joe has,' the boy said cryptically. 'He's always talking about you—'

'I'd better be getting on,' Anne said hastily, making her retreat. 'Bye!'

The boy merely grunted and turned his head away again, and Anne passed on, noting with an absent curse the dirt under her nails where she had been scratching the bull. They hadn't bothered to groom him for the sale, that was obvious.

Even apart from the smell, you could tell when you were coming to the pig section of the market by the noise. All pigs screamed on principle whenever they were touched, and once they'd started, they would scream even before they were touched simply whenever anyone came near them. To the uninitiated, it would have seemed from a distance that they were being butchered there and then, by the noise they were making, whereas in fact they were only being driven from one pen to another.

The trouble was that three of the smaller pig-farms shared a lorry. The pigs from each farm were daubed with a different colour – red, green, and blue – and by the dab of colour on their rumps they could be identified. They were all unloaded together into one large pen, and from this pen they had to be rounded up and driven into separate pens according to colour. It was a system that saved the farmers a lot of money on transport, but it was heavy on labour. The obstinate, panicking pigs were the hardest things on earth to handle, and usually all the stockmen and

37

boys ended up giving a hand, whatever farm they belonged to.

Here Anne found Joe, taking his turn at trying to corner the last few red weaners from among the greens and blues and drive them through the gate. A boy was stationed at the gate, ready to slip it open at the right moment, and shut it before all the others dashed through as well, while Joe, with a large piece of cardboard in his left hand, did the cutting-out.

There was a ring of spectators round the outside of the pen, and Anne joined them. Some of them were shoppers and trippers, but most of them were stockmen and farmers, come to watch the fun – it was a kind of local rodeo. The boys were sent in first, when there were still so many pigs in the enclosure that they couldn't move about much, but as the pen emptied and the pigs had more room to manoeuvre, the more experienced handlers tried their luck. It was a sign of Joe's status among his fellows that he was in there now trying to get the last two out.

Anne slipped quietly into a place on the rails and watched. Joe looked the part all right, she thought, broad and powerful with his suntanned face and arms, his shirt sleeves rolled up to the elbow, his corduroy working pants tucked into heavy dunlops and secured round the middle with binder-twine. His eyes were bright with humour, his mouth firm with concentration; his big hands looked capable but kind. Anne felt a surge of affection for him as she watched.

The little red pig he was after had run himself into a corner and had burrowed his head in among the other pigs in the manner of an ostrich. Joe stalked forward, and as the other pigs shifted uneasily away, the red pig looked over his shoulder and rolled his eyes with alarm, keeping his behind towards the enemy as if it were a sure defence.

'Go on, Joe!' 'You got 'im Joe!' the onlookers cried. Joe stalked the pig carefully, and then slid the cardboard sheet between its body and the railings and reached with his right hand for its ear. His fingers were within a hair's breadth of the ear when the little pig made a bolt for it, straight between Joe's legs, sending him flying over backwards to land sitting in the mud. The onlookers roared delightedly, and Joe grinned aimiably and shrugged his shoulders. He would never lose his temper with a pig, no matter how infuriating it was. That was why he was such a good pigman.

Patiently he got up and began to stalk his quarry all over again, following it calmly until he had driven it into a corner for the final grab. The stockmen were cheering him wildly now, and laying odds on the pig for another escape. Joe made his cutting-out movement again, and again the desperate and perverse animal flung himself at Joe's legs for the break-out. This time Joe was quicker. Grinning broadly he abandoned his cardboard and grabbed the pig with both arms, and, before it had time to wriggle free, he had taken its tail in one hand and one of its ears in the other, and was running it on three legs towards the gate.

The pig squealed hysterically as if it were being

murdered, and Anne heard a woman in a smart hat murmur something about cruelty to animals. As soon as the creature was through the gate, however, Joe released it, and it stopped screaming at once and began snuffling around the mud like the others, looking for something to eat.

'Well done, Joe,' Anne called with the others, and he must have picked out her voice, for he turned his head and smiled, then came over to her, calling over his shoulder,

'All right, Tom, I've done my bit. You can sort the rest of your blessed pigs out yourself.'

Then, smiling broadly, he climbed out of the pen to greet Anne.

'Hello,' he said. 'You're looking very beautiful, as usual.'

'Hello, Joe. You're looking very muddy as usual,' she replied.

'Well, I can't help it,' he began, and she patted his shoulder.

'I'm joking. Listen, are you ready to come for a cup of tea and a sandwich? I'm starving, and I know you must be.'

'Yes, O.K., but you must come and see Rosemary first. She's here with her litter, and you've never actually seen her, have you?'

'Not in the flesh,' Anne said. 'Though I saw a photo of her in the paper at the County Show. And you never stop talking about her.'

'She's wonderful,' Joe said, his eyes shining with pleasure. 'Come and see.'

In comparative quiet the sows stood in private pens under cover a little way from the other pigs, and it was evident even at first glance that

Rosemary was the biggest sow of the lot. It always amazed Anne how big a pig could be. Rosemary was huge, and filled her pen entirely, so that she couldn't have turned round if she wanted, though it was difficult imagining this massive mountain of pink flesh wanting anything other than to step out of the weight of flesh and be a slender young pigling again.

Around her her large family minced and teetered on their tiny pointed feet, like fat ladies on very high heels. The young of almost every species has its charm, and Anne thought the piglets were adorable.

'So small and pink,' she said. 'Really quite huggable.'

'Isn't she lovely,' Joe said, scarcely aware of what she had said. Rosemary snuffled at his foot with her wet snout, and peered up at him from under her shady ears, looking almost coy about it. 'What a specimen! What a breeder! And not a runt among them. She's a queen – aren't you, old lady?'

'She's certainly big,' Anne said, not wanting to be ungenerous. Joe scratched Rosemary's back with an iron gate-pin, and Rosemary sighed happily and grunted as the dried mud flaked off. Her numerous offspring seethed along her side, suckling, lined up like people in a canteen queue.

'Anyone can see,' Anne said, 'why piglets are narrower at the front than at the back. It's the only way they'd all fit in. Anyway, watching them is making me hungry. If I agree she's the most remarkable pig in the world, can we go and get a sandwich?'

41

'Of course, I'm sorry. I should have thought. You've been working all morning,' Joe said, starting back to reality. 'Come on then, we'll see what we can get. Did you have a nice day?'

He was all attention at once, and escorted her in a courtly manner towards Ted's Teas and Snacks, the tea-hut the stockmen favoured. It was a wooden hut on a raised floor – raised above possible flooding, Anne had always supposed – with wooden benches and tables like a school refectory, and a counter at the far end. They sold tea and coffee, sandwiches and snacks, and the best sausage rolls in Dorset. Anne slipped into a place on the end of a bench while Joe went up to order, and the eight old farm-hands seated along the bench all slid up silently to make room for her.

Joe came back with their order on a battered tin tray – two hot sausage rolls and baked beans, and tea in huge white mugs that looked like shaving mugs – and edged in on the end of the bench with a cordial smile at the old men.

'There you are, my duck,' he said, serving Anne. 'I can't stay long, but I ought to be able to get off a bit early today, once I've seen Rosemary off.' He looked a bit bleak. 'I don't know what the place is going to be like without her. It'll seem bare, somehow.'

'You'll miss her,' Anne said. 'I must try somehow to make up to you for her.'

'You couldn't replace her,' Joe said, and for the life of her, Anne couldn't tell if he was joking or not. 'Anyway, what would you like to do this evening? Say I get through about half past four, have a bit of a wash, I could be ready around five.'

'How about getting something to eat, and then going to the fair,' Anne suggested. Joe looked doubtful.

'Is that really what you want to do?'

'I wouldn't have said it if I didn't mean it,' Anne said. 'Why not, anyway?'

'It's a bit rough and noisy, isn't it? People shoving you around, and picking your pockets, and swearing and all that sort of thing. Wouldn't you like to go somewhere a bit quieter?'

'No,' Anne said firmly. 'I've had a quiet week. I'd like to go somewhere a bit noisy.'

'But—'

'Joe, I'm not made of cotton wool,' she said crossly. 'I can stand a bit of shoving as well as the next person. If you had your way I'd. be locked up in a tower somewhere with a spinning wheel.'

Joe looked hurt. 'I don't mean to stop you enjoying yourself,' he said. 'It's just that I always think of you as – well, something a bit precious, to be cared for. You're not like the other girls, rushing round in trousers and leather jackets and smoking and swearing like men. You're – a lady.'

Anne felt ashamed of her ill temper, and reached out to touch his hand. 'I'm sorry Joe, I shouldn't snap at you. Of course I love to be treated as a lady. It's just that – well, I want some fun, sometimes, too.'

'I'm sorry,' he said miserably. 'I know I'm a bit dull. I don't know why you bother with me, really. I've often wondered—'

43

From anyone else it would have been self-pity, and worthy of a kick in the pants, but Anne knew that Joe meant it, that he really didn't know why she bothered with him. He thought she was too good for him, whereas, if he knew what she was really like, he would know he was a whole lot too good for *her*.

'Don't,' she said, and he stopped obediently. 'Can we go to the fair tonight, Joe? I've a childish liking for fairgrounds. I grew out of circuses, but I never quite grew out of fairs.'

'Of course we can,' he said. 'Anything you like.'

'And Wendy will be there – she said to tell you that there's bowling for a pig—'

She had meant it as a joke, but when she saw him smile with pleasure at the thought, she hadn't the heart to go on. Wendy was a little too close to being right and Anne was a little too close to feeling superior to Joe. It wouldn't do.

While Joe went back to work, Anne spent a happy afternoon wandering about the market. She had one or two bits of shopping to do for herself and for Dad, but for the rest she was content just to browse, to observe, and to bargain-hunt. There were still stalls where you could bargain for goods, and things like pairs of tights and face-cream never came amiss. There was the 'dead-stock' auction, where you could buy a chest of drawers or a wheelbarrow or a cast-iron mangle or 150 feet of hosepipe; the provisions section, where the fruit and vegetables and eggs and meat were sold, and where towards the end of the day odd 'mixed lots' were sold and you might end up with five stone of potatoes, three dozen eggs, four boiling fowls, and a huge box of winter store-apples, all for a fiver.

Out of duty to Dad she paid a visit to the small livestock market, where they sold pigeons and chickens and goats and cagebirds and, inevitably, rabbits. Greys and albinos and long-haired blacks; ruby eyes and brown eyes and thousands of whiffling noses. She had to admit that the baby rabbits were sweet, but then, so were the baby pigs. What with Dad and his rabbits and Joe and his pigs – it was no wonder they got on so well together, she thought. She had read somewhere that women always chose men who remind them of their fathers. Was that why she had chosen Joe? Strange though. But then, she had not chosen Joe; he had chosen her, if anyone other than Fate could have been said to have had a hand in it.

At the edge of the area a coster's cart was piled high with chicken coops, and a goat and two kids – obviously a purchase – were tethered to its wheel, waiting for their owner to come back. A smartly dressed man was sitting on one of the shafts, evidently a town visitor taking a rest. His back was to Anne, and also to the goats – a fatal mistake, for the adult goat had enough slack on the rope to reach him, and was thoughtfully nibbling at the tail of his jacket.

He hadn't noticed yet, and nor had anyone else, Anne saw, looking round. Serve him right, she thought, and was about to pass on when the man turned his head slightly, and she saw from the three-quarters profile that it was the handsome stranger she and Wendy had noticed that morning. Hardly knowing why that made any difference, she changed tack and walked across to him, calling.

'Hi, look out! You're being eaten.'

It was a moment before the man realised she was addressing him, and then he glanced back, saw the goat, and jumped up with a muffled curse. One or two people caught the tail end of the drama and laughed, while the man twisted round, trying to inspect the damage. Anne reassured him.

'It's all right, you caught it in time – it's only sucked, not chewed.'

'Thank heavens for that,' he said, but he smiled and made light of it. 'Next time I will know better than to sit near a goat. Thanks for warning me.'

'That's all right,' Anne said. Close to she saw that his face was not really handsome: his nose was not straight, and his mouth curled up one side more than the other, and his chin was the wrong shape – but it was strangely attractive, and his eyes – level grey eyes under dark brows – were certainly striking. It was a face you couldn't help but be interested in. 'Goats will eat anything, and they don't distinguish between old rope and gents' natty suiting. But it should clean all right.'

'Oh, no damage done, not to worry,' he said. He was taking it very calmly, she thought, considering what that suit must have cost him. Then, as if he had divined her thought, he said,

46

'Serve me right for wearing this here, anyway.' The goat stared up at him with her strange yellow eyes and then lifted her lip in a contemptuous expression. 'Sorry to interrupt your dinner, old man,' he said.

'Actually, it's a female,' Anne said, and then, since there didn't seem to be anything else to say, she nodded a brief goodbye and walked on. Wait until I tell Wendy, she thought, that I've actually spoken to her Martini advert, not to mention saved him from a dreadful fate!

At five Anne went to meet Joe outside the Black Bear, the large AA hotel on the corner of the market square. Joe was as punctual as ever, and she saw his familiar figure waiting for her on the steps from across the road. Not tall, but broad-set, strong shoulders and arms, his fair hair thick and ruffled, his face firm and tanned – he was good looking enough to please any girl; but with the image of the handsome stranger fresh in her mind, Anne gave an inward sigh at the sight of that same old shapeless check jacket, the plain white shirt, open at the neck, and the grey flannel trousers. She knew them all so well!

Anne tried to keep herself smartly dressed, though there was not an enormous selection in Market Winton. There were the usual chain stores, and one or two small boutiques, and by ringing the changes between the two sources, she managed to look not only smart, but individual. Joe, to do him justice, always noticed her clothes, and complimented her on her appearance, but it never seemed to occur to him to do anything about his.

No, that was hardly fair; he was saving up for the day when he'd be able to buy his own place, and in any case, a stockman's wage was not of the highest. But it was true that he didn't see any point in spending money on clothes. He had one suit, for weddings and funerals, as the local saying was, and his 'good' trousers and jacket, and as long as he looked clean and well-pressed, he didn't see the point in having a choice of clothes. With another small sigh, Anne crossed the road to meet him.

'Hello, there you are,' he greeted her, and his face lit up with a smile. 'I don't know about you, but I'm starving.'

'Me too,' said Anne, slipping her hand through his arm. 'Where shall we go to eat?'

Joe squeezed her hand against his ribs and they started down the street. 'Well, what about the Forum? I don't think you can do better, really,' he said. Anne made a face.

'You always say that. And we always eat there. Couldn't we go somewhere else?'

'Well, like where for instance?' Joe asked. 'There's only the Wimpy Bar apart from that, and I don't think you get such good value there.'

'Well, what about a restaurant for a change? What about that Italian place down in Castle Street? It looks awfully nice from the outside.'

Joe shook his head. 'Well, I don't know,' he said slowly. 'I know it looks smart, but you have to pay for that sort of thing. The prices are bound to be higher, and Italian food is cheap stuff sold dear.'

'But just for a change!' Anne cried.

48

'I think we'd better stick to the good old Forum,' Joe said, nodding. 'I know it's not much to look at, but the food's all right and you get good big portions there – much better value really.'

'Oh, is that all you think about?' Anne cried. 'The Forum's no better than a transport café!'

'Well what's wrong with a transport café?' Joe asked, puzzled. 'You just pay fancy prices in other places for the same food.'

'Just for once you could splash out,' Anne said. 'Just for once you could live a little!'

'I *am* saving, you know,' Joe rebuked her gently.

'Then let me pay,' Anne said. 'Or at least let me pay the extra. I don't object to spending my money.'

There was a brief silence, and she saw a white line etch itself round Joe's lips. She had hit him where it hurt, and despite her anger, she was sorry. They walked on in silence for a moment, and then began speaking at once.

'I don't take a girl out, and then let her pay,' Joe said.

'I only wanted a change,' Anne said. Joe stopped for her to go on. She said, rather shame-facedly, 'A transport café might be all right, but it isn't much of a treat, is it, to take a girl on her night out?'

'I'm sorry, Anne,' Joe said. They had been walking on all this time in the direction of the Forum, but he veered away now, pulling her with him. 'We'll go to the Italian place.'

Anne pulled her arm free and stopped in the

middle of the pavement, and Joe turned back to look at her in surprise. Anne could not be sure if he was genuinely surprised, or if he was only acting dumb, but in either case she was exasperated, and told him so.

'Oh for God's sake, Joe, what's the good now? I don't want to go there now. Let's go to the Forum for heaven's sake and get it over with.'

'I don't understand. A moment ago you said . . .'

'I know what I said,' she shouted at him. 'I wouldn't have any pleasure in it now. If you're going to give in to me, why don't you do it straight away, instead of taking all the pleasure out of it first by arguing, and then giving in when I don't want it any more?'

'Want what?' Joe asked.

'Whatever it was I wanted!' Anne raved. Even through her rage, she could see the funny side of it, and however much she wanted to tear her hair, she also wanted to laugh. At length she took a deep breath and said in what she hoped was a reasonable voice,

'I know you're saving, and I know you don't like to spend my money, but just once in a while it does people good to splash out on something that isn't totally necessary, just rather nice. And now,' she finished, putting her hand through his arm again, 'let's go to the Forum and forget I ever spoke.'

Joe went with her, but she could see he was still puzzled, and he was more silent even than usual through the meal, evidently thinking something out. Joe had sausages, egg and chips, and Anne, out of self-indulgence, had a mixed grill, which was the best thing that the Forum did, and not at all bad, but she didn't enjoy it. When they had finished, Joe said.

'Do you still want to go to the fair?'

'We might as well,' Anne said, but the fun had gone out of it. Her evening was spoilt, she felt, and it was for such a silly thing. She felt out of temper with Joe, dissatisfied with her lot, and above all guilty that she should feel either out of temper or dissatisfied. Even the cheerful noise of the fairground and the nostalgic smell of the diesel engines and the candyfloss and the donkeys did little to lift her spirits. They met up with Wendy and Graham, and Wendy asked Joe if he had bowled for the pig yet, and rather laboured the joke until Anne told her, sourly to shut up.

It was a good fair, and as they wandered round, content at first just to look until the atmosphere built up, Anne felt herself cheering up. There was something, after all, about a fair, a contrast between the illusion of luxury and the reality of squalor behind it, and a sense of total extravagance that was quite charming. The lights, the gold paint, the wheezy music, the hoarse tempting cries, the promise of purely temporary delight, all added their own allure to the scene. Anne drank it all in, and found herself smiling again.

Joe, however, was still unhappy, and perhaps dwelling on Anne's concealed accusation of meanness, kept trying to persuade her to go on everything they passed. It was as if his money was burning holes in his pockets. Anne was content to watch. She went on the roundabout and the waltzer, but preferred to watch Wendy and Graham on the caterpillar and the dodgems, despite Joe's urging at her elbow. They ended up buying four hot dogs, and finding some caravan steps out of the throng where they could sit and eat them.

'It's a good fair, isn't it?' Wendy said through a mouthful of bun.

'Terrible waste of money,' Graham said cheerfully. Joe looked as though he agreed, but not cheerfully.

'What isn't?' Anne said, trying to be diplomatic. 'Hey, Wendy, you'll never guess who I saw this afternoon.'

'How many guesses?' she asked.

'Don't be silly.'

'All right, I'll have three. The Pope, Prince Charles, and the man we saw in the café this morning.'

'How did you know?'

'I saw him too – I was going to tell you,' Wendy said. 'He must be staying in town somewhere, I think. Can't see him in a boarding house, leave alone a camp site, so he must be at one of the hotels.'

'Who's this?' Graham asked.

'Your successor,' Wendy said, laughing.

'My successor in what?'

'In taking me out. I should think he's got pots of money.'

'He's welcome to you,' Graham said emphatically, and she made a face at him. 'I say, Joe, you're very quiet. I don't think you've enjoyed yourself at all this evening.'

'Bit tired,' Joe said. He stared down at his

half-eaten hot dog with distaste, and then threw it into the nearest waste-paper bin. 'Look,' he said, 'I don't want to drag Anne away when she's having a good time, but I'd really like to go home. Would you give her a lift home for me?'

'Of course,' Graham was saying with surprise, when Anne interrupted.

'No, it's all right, I'm ready to go home now. I've seen all I want to see.'

Joe looked at her doubtfully, but she returned his gaze steadily, and at length he nodded.

'Just as you like,' he said. 'Cheerio, Wendy, Graham. See you again.'

'Bye, Joe. Bye Anne.'

'I'll give you a ring tomorrow at the office, Anne,' Wendy called after her. Anne knew what that was for – to discuss Joe's mood. She fell in beside him, and they walked in silence for the privileged place in the market where Joe left the van.

Joe held the door for her as courteously as ever as she settled herself on the blanket on the tattered front seat, but on the short drive back to Winton Parva she felt the atmosphere thick as soup inside the van. When they pulled up at the station, Joe said quickly,

'I won't come in, if you don't mind.'

'Oh please, Dad always like to see you,' Anne said. There was a brief silence.

'Give your Dad my apologies, would you, but I'd like to get home.' He seemed to be waiting for her to get out. Was that all? No goodnight kiss, no smile or touch of the hand. Anne knew whose fault it was.

'Joe, listen, I'm sorry for getting ratty with you—'

'There's nothing to apologise for,' he said.

'Oh come on, don't be like that!'

'Like what?'

'All sniffy and proud. I said I'm sorry.'

'And I said there's nothing to apologise for. I mean it.' He sounded quite firm and sincere. Anne was silent for a moment.

'You don't understand,' she began, but Joe stopped her, touching the back of her hand briefly.

'I understand, maybe better than you think,' he said. There seemed to be no more to come, so feeling very much at sea, Anne bid him good-night and got out of the car, and Joe drove away without another word.

'Isn't Joe with you, love?' Dad asked as she came in. She swallowed, and smiled.

'He felt rather tired, Dad, so he went straight home. He sent you his love,' she said. She could see that her father was puzzled by this, for it was not like Joe, and she added off the top of her head, 'To tell you a secret, I think he was a bit upset to see Rosemary go.'

'Rosemary! Don't tell me they've sold his prize sow.'

'Yes, and her litter. They fetched a good price.'

'I'll bet they did. But it's no wonder he's depressed. He thought the world of that pig.' Dad said, nodding wisely. How very true, Anne thought, and put the kettle on.

Four

'Letter for you, Dad,' Anne said, coming in with the mail as her father sat down to breakfast.

'Another bill, I'll be bound,' he said, holding out his hand for it. She held it back, teasingly.

'No. Guess again.'

'A circular then? A catalogue.'

'No. You're a rotten guesser.'

'Well I give up then. Oh, it's a letter all right. Now who could be writing to me?'

'British Rail,' Anne said, watching him slit open the envelope with his horny, ridged thumbnail.

'How do you know?' he asked her, astonished. She smiled sweetly.

'It says on the envelope. Look, at the bottom: If undelivered, return to—'

'So it does. How clever of you.'

'Well, what does it say?' she prompted impatiently. She watched his face as he read the letter, frowned, and then went back to the beginning to read it again. Not good news, then, or not wholly good. He came to the end and looked up at her, and then passed her the letter, saying.

'Here, you'd better read this.'

'"Dear Mr Symons,"' she read, '"With regard to your recent request for repairs to be carried out to the roof of your dwelling" – did you, Dad? I didn't know.'

'Yes, a couple of weeks ago. You know where that tile came off. I patched it up, but it wasn't a permanent job. Go on.'

'"—roof of your dwelling, we have decided, in view of the general condition of the building, that it would be uneconomical to make any further repairs or improvements. We have pleasure therefore in offering you an alternative dwelling, namely no. 3, Pear Tree Close, London Road, Market Winton." That's those new bungalows, isn't it, Dad, on the main road going towards Magna? What's this all about?' The rest of the letter dealt with a description of the 'alternative dwelling' and what Dad had to do to signify his consent. 'They won't make us go, will they?'

'I'm afraid they will,' Dad said. 'I'd heard some rumours on the wind about a change coming, but I never thought it would affect us directly, not like this. You see, you know it's only the army that keeps this branch line alive?'

'Of course,' Anne nodded. 'People can say what they like about the army spoiling the countryside and the soldiers getting drunk in the local pubs, but if the army hadn't built a camp at Leabourne, they would have shut old Parva station years ago.'

'That's right,' Dad said. 'Well, I get all the army gossip from the blokes on the transports while they wait for the trains to come in, and it seems that for some time the army have been intending to build on to the camp at Leabourne and open an experimental tank station, for testing new weapons and tanks and so on.'

'But what's that got to do with us?' Anne was puzzled.

'A bigger camp means more soldiers, and that means more traffic on our branch. And more houses for the married men, and more people using the station. Now Winton Parva's all right for the amount of traffic it handles, but if there's going to be three or four times the number of people passing through, the station won't do at all. Oh no, not at all.' Dad shook his head, and his eyes were reflective.

'I haven't seen the plans,' he went on, 'but I can imagine it pretty well. They did the same thing at Wool. A new entry hall, new station buildings – ticket office and toilets and so on. And a big concrete area in front for the cars and the transports and the BRS vans.'

'Over our bit of waste-ground,' Anne said, suddenly understanding. 'And our house will be in the way.'

'That's right,' Dad said. 'It's an old house: no proper damp course, and sinking one side anyway because of the sewers. They wouldn't bother to patch it up when they're going to pull it down in a couple of years anyway.'

'But if they move us, what about your job?' Anne cried. 'They can't have a residential station master who lives a couple of miles away.'

'Extra staff,' Dad said. 'Extra traffic would mean extra staff. Not residential any more; it'd be shifts. They'd bring in a younger man, maybe two, to share the shifts with me. And then, the next thing you know, they'd be making me redundant. "Poor old boy with a dummy leg" they'd say. "He can't manage – pension him off!"'

'Nonsense, Dad,' Anne said robustly. 'Your foot makes no difference, and you know it. Come on, it isn't like you to be glum. You should be proud that they're upgrading your station. You always said it was too quiet.'

Dad smiled faintly. 'I used to say it, but I liked it quiet really. But – leaving here! You've lived here nearly all your life. Your mother spent her last days here. And to turn us out and put us in one of those nasty red-brick bungalows. Pah!' He made a face.

'Well, it needn't be for a year or two, need it? I mean, it doesn't say in the letter that they'll make us go.'

'No, it makes it sound like we've got a choice, all very polite and nice, but they'll find ways. Won't repair the roof, for a start.'

'Well, we could manage,' Anne began, but her father went on.

'It would be a relief to me if you'd get yourself married and settled down in a place of your own. I wouldn't mind what happened, then, if it was only myself I had to worry about.'

'You don't have to worry about me.'

'Oh yes I do. I'm your father. And what about you and Joe?'

'*What* about me and Joe?'

'Did you have a quarrel last night?'

'I told you—'

'Yes, I know what you told me, but I got to thinking it over last night after you'd gone to bed, and I don't think Joe would be that upset over a pig. I know he's mad about them, but he cares more for you than for any pig in this world.'

'Are you sure about that, Dad?' Anne said quietly. 'I'm not sure. I think pigs come first with him.'

'So you did have a quarrel.'

'No, of course not.'

'All right, I know it's none of my business, and I won't ask you any more. But think about this: Joe's a good steady lad, nothing flighty about him, and as honest as the day is long. You'll go a long way to find a man as steady and honest as him.'

Anne said nothing, but she thought, perhaps that's just the trouble. He's too steady. A girl needs a bit of fun now and then. But she didn't want to upset Dad on top of his bad news, so she smiled and pretended to agree with him, so that by the time she left for work he had forgotten their quarrel.

It seemed to be the day for news. When Mr Cass came in and had read through his mail, he called out to Anne,

'Would you come in for a moment, Miss Symons?' Anne took her notepad and pen, but it was not for dictation that she was wanted. Mr Cass twinkled gravely at her and told her to sit down.

'Miss Symons, it hasn't escaped my attention that you take what I might call a scholarly interest in the cases that the firm handles, so it will be old knowledge to you that we took over various cases from Comar and Sons when they went out of business, and among them the Trusteeship of the Bowyer Estate.'

Anne nodded. 'Yes, sir. And the Bowyer Estate—'

'Just so. The Bowyer Estate incorporates the piece of land in which our client Mr Halderthay is interested.'

'You've had some news on it?' Anne asked eagerly. Mr Cass smiled.

'That particular piece of land is to be sold, and as Trustees we can choose either to place the sale with an estate agent, or sell the land privately. I see no reason why Mr Halderthay should not be offered first refusal before the land is offered for sale publicly, do you?'

'That's marvellous,' Anne said, 'but—'

'But why am I telling you?' That wasn't what Anne had been going to say. She had been about to say, but he may not be able to afford it yet, but he had been saving for four years, after all. Mr Cass went on, 'It has not escaped my notice that you are quite well acquainted with Mr Halderthay, one might almost say *friendly*' – the eyes twinkled again, 'and I thought you might like to have the pleasure of breaking the news to him yourself.'

'Thank you very much,' Anne said. 'It was very kind of you.'

It was kind to think of it, but Anne, as she went back to her own office, could only wish it had happened a day earlier, before she and Joe had – she could hardly say quarrelled, for it didn't amount to that. But before the little coldness that had sprung up between them. It occurred

60

to her that when they parted last night, they hadn't made any arrangement to meet on Saturday, which was the other night they generally went out. It might have been an accidental omission, or it might have been the cold shoulder. Perhaps she deserved it, but if Joe was deliberately leaving her in doubt, it was not like him, and she would be justified in being angry and offended.

She had no way of contacting Joe, which was the main reason why they made their arrangements for the next time when they said goodnight. Well, she wouldn't judge him too quickly; she would wait to see if he got in touch with her. He might telephone her at the office – he knew the number – or he might make occasion to come into town during the day and drop by to speak to her. Or he might call round to the house tonight. She would wait and see what happened; but she couldn't help feeling uneasy.

She was just taking five minutes break at eleven o'clock to drink her coffee and read a page or two of her book, when the outer door opened, and she looked up quickly, thinking it was Joe. Had she stopped to analyse her reaction, it might have told her quite a lot about her feelings for Joe, but she had not time to think about that, for it was not Joe who came in from the street, but the dark stranger of yesterday.

'Good morning,' he began, 'I was wondering,' and then he saw who it was. His mouth curled up at one side in a funny, lopsided smile. 'Well, if it isn't the lady who knows about goats!'

'Goats, pigs, cows, even rabbits,' she said

61

briskly, not to let him have it all his own way. 'You name it – I recognise it.'

He smiled in appreciation of the sally. His grey eyes scrutinised her steadily and Anne caught herself think-again that, while not handsome in the conventional sense, he was certainly very attractive . . .

'We seem to be fated to meet,' he was saying. 'I should have known when I chose a solicitors' firm at random, I would be directed in my choice by some mysterious force.'

'Do you always talk like this?' she marvelled. He frowned at her.

'I have you at a distinct disadvantage,' he said seriously. 'You see, I can say anything I like to you, but you have to be polite to me, because I'm a potential customer, and the customer's always right.'

'But as against that,' Anne said equally seriously, 'I'm a lady, and you have to be polite to me whatever position you're in.'

'In that case, Miss—'

'Symons.'

'In that case, Miss Symons, we shall have a delightfully polite relationship. I can see grave problems, however, whenever we reach a door. We shall both be standing back insisting the other goes first.'

Anne laughed. 'What makes you so sure we are going to have a relationship?' she asked.

'I don't see how we can avoid it,' he said. His eyes found hers, and held them, and she felt her heart beating a little more quickly than it should at the words. Then he went on, 'After all, any

62

two people saying anything to each other are having a relationship of some sort, though it may be the merest formal exchange.'

Anne cursed herself inwardly for having made too much of too little. She said with a formal smile.

'Do I take it that you wish to make an appointment to see one of the partners?'

'You do. It's on a matter of conveyancing. I want to buy a building and plot of land in the high street, and I need someone to handle the sale for me.'

Anne's mind flooded with questions and speculations at that point. Was he acting as an agent or buying for himself? With what purpose? Was it a house or a business? She racked her brains to remember what buildings were up for sale in the high street, but couldn't remember a single one. If he was buying for himself, it looked as though he was well-off, and perhaps it also meant that he would be staying, settling down in Market Winton. This in its turn threatened to set off an even more disturbing chain of questions in her mind, and she had been sitting staring at him for several seconds already. She must not slip from her professional perfection. She put her questions aside and said.

'May I have your name, please? I'll see if one of the partners can see you now.'

'Oh it needn't be right now if it isn't convenient. I can come in at any time. I'm staying at the Black Bear, just round the corner. But of course you'd know where it is.'

'Of course,' Anne agreed. 'And the name?'

'My card,' he said, slipping one out of his breast pocket with such a practiced air that it was evident he did it many times a day. He must be a business man, she decided, to carry cards round with him; but the card told her nothing. It was quite plain, simply with the name printed across the middle, and an address in the bottom right hand corner. 'M. F. Conrad' it said. '221 Regent Street, London W.1.'

'I won't keep you a moment, Mr Conrad,' Anne said in her most professional manner, and slipped into Mr Whetlore's room, but her thoughts were very unprofessional. 'Wait till I tell Wendy that I know his name,' she thought, and, 'I wonder what the M. F. stands for?'

She was back in a moment, still holding the card. 'Mr Whetlore would be happy to see you at any time this afternoon,' she told him.

'What time do you make the tea?' he asked abruptly. She was so surprised that she stumbled over her answer.

'Oh – er – about three, usually.'

'Then I'll come at two-thirty,' he said, and with a debonair smile bid her 'Good morning!' and was gone, leaving Anne to wonder if he meant to be there for tea, or to miss it.

Anne stayed in the office over her lunch-hour in case Joe should call, but by two-thirty, when M. F. Conrad came back for his appointment, she had neither seen nor heard anything of Joe. She showed the client in to Mr Whetlore, and went back to her desk, and there sat for some time, staring at the visiting card and speculating idly.

Maurice Fitzroy? Martin Frank? how about Montmorency Featherstonehaugh? A business man, obviously, but of what sort? He looked like an accountant, or perhaps a solicitor, except that he was just slightly too glamorous, just a little too showy. She found herself remembering the moment when their eyes met, and shook the thought away as a horse shakes off a fly. Whatever else he was, he was probably a smooth worker, and she shouldn't allow herself to be taken in by his ready charm.

She was taken by surprise when the door of Mr Whetlore's office opened long before she would have expected them to be finished. It was still only ten to three – he wouldn't get his tea after all. Or perhaps, if he had intended to avoid tea-time, she should say he had just made it in time. She smiled formally as he stopped in front of her desk, and said.

'Everything satisfactory, Mr Conrad?'

'Perfectly thank you, Miss Symons.' Then suddenly he leaned both hands on her desk, smiled winningly at her, and asked, 'What are you doing tonight?'

Anne was taken aback, not having expected so abrupt a proposition. 'That's a very bold question,' she said.

'What should I have said?'

'What should *I* say now?'

'Well, it seems to me you have two possibilities. Possibility (a) – you can tell me to mind my own business. Possibility (b) – you can tell me what you're doing tonight.'

Anne thought about it. 'Possibility (b)

subsection one – I can tell you what I'm really doing tonight. Possibility (b) subsection two – I can tell you a lie.'

'But in that case,' he said, 'you would simply be telling me to mind my own business in a roundabout way, so that's covered by possibility (a). Which is it to be?'

'I'm lost after all those possibilities,' Anne said, playing for time. He was not fooled.

'Mind my own business, eh? Well, I should have expected you to be spoken for,' he said. Anne would have liked to have asked why, but feared it might be construed as fishing. 'Perhaps some other time, as they say on the films. You might tell me, however—'

'Yes?' Anne was prepared to be helpful, since she was off the hook.

'What is there to do on Saturday night for a single man with no attachments; at least, not yet.'

'There's the discotheque in the Castle Hotel,' Anne said, furrowing her brow as if in thought, 'or there's the Young Farmers' Ball at Springbourne.'

'I'm never sure just exactly how polite you're being,' he said suspiciously. 'However, on this occasion I've no doubt as to which you'll be attending.'

'Why is that?' Anne asked.

'Because the van I saw you getting into last night was undoubtedly a Young Farmer's vehicle.'

'You saw me last night? You saw me at the fair?'

'I saw you at the fair.'

66

'Then you must know I am spoken for. You didn't need to ask.'

'Not necessarily,' he said, looking at her judiciously. 'You were accompanied it's true by a good-looking young man, but you'd evidently had words with him, so there was a good chance you might be available.'

'You seem to have taken a great deal of notice of my private affairs.' Anne frowned.

'My dear Miss Symons,' he said coolly, 'Anything you do in public can hardly be classed as your private affairs.' He straightened up, unruffled. 'Anyway, enjoy the Young Farmers' Ball. No doubt I shall be seeing you again.'

Anne stuck her tongue out at his retreating back. Not very professional conduct, but it relieved her feelings a little. She was not used to being bested in verbal combat. The door had hardly closed behind him, when a peevish call from Mr Whetlore reminded her that she had not made the tea, or even, as yet, put the kettle on.

There was no call from Joe during the afternoon, nor by the time she was ready to go home; though she still had the evening to expect a visit from him, Anne had a feeling she was not going to be contacted. She didn't know whether she had hurt his feelings, or whether he was staying away because he felt he bored her, but whichever was the real reason, it was not a happy thought. She was very fond of Joe – he was kind, and good, and she didn't want him to be hurt. Apart from anything else, they had been going out together for a very long time, and sheer habit made it hard to imagine life, or even a weekend, without him.

Then there was Dad to think about. He held Joe in high esteem, and his dearest wish was that Anne should get married and settled down. It would near break Dad's heart if he knew she and Joe had quarrelled. It would be hard to keep it from him, too; not only was there Saturday night, when she and Joe usually went out, to be got over, but Monday was the Bank Holiday. That was why the fair was there, of course, though the significance had escaped her until now. But it would seem very odd if with both Sunday and Monday free she did not go out with Joe at all, and Joe did not even come over for tea.

She ought to explain to Dad straight away when she got home, she thought, as she cycled through the town; explain that they hadn't really quarrelled, just had a slight misunderstanding. That way Dad wouldn't make too much of it. When she arrived home, however, Dad greeted her with an affectionate kiss, asked her how her day had been, told her she must be tired, and added.

'I've got tea all ready for us both, so you can just sit yourself straight down. I expect you're glad it's the Bank Holiday on Monday. Have you and Joe got anything planned for Monday?'

'No, we haven't planned anything,' Anne said with perfect truth. Now was the moment, but somehow she just couldn't say it.

'Oh well, that might be for the best anyway,' Dad said. 'You never know what the weather will be like, do you?'

Saturday got used up, as it always did, with shopping and bits of neglected housework, and letter-writing, and various bits of hand-washing and mending that needed catching up on. Saturday was Dad's busy day in the station, with extra trains laid on for holiday-makers, and extra tickets bought by soldiers going out for the day and home for weekend leave, so they didn't see much of each other. Anne told herself she did not expect Joe to call, but whenever a car passed in the road outside she found herself stiffening to listen. In the afternoon she gave in to herself and took a bucket of water and cleaned the downstairs windows so that she could keep an eye on the road, but he did not come.

If I stay in tonight, she told herself, Dad is sure to ask why. On the other hand, if I go and Joe comes round . . .? And if I go out and Dad sees me taking the bus . . .? Life seemed fraught with problems until suddenly, she decided to stop worrying about them.

'Joe can't expect me to wait round for him without a word of a message,' she told herself severely. 'Anyway, it would do us both good to go out with someone else once in a while. We're getting stale and narrow-minded.'

The problem of being seen leaving under her own steam was easily overcome simply by starting off when Dad was across at the station, leaving a note for him in the kitchen, propped up against the tea-caddy, the first place he would look.

'Gone out – back late. Don't wait up for me,' it said. Just what she always said. He would wait up, of course; he always did.

Anne took her bike and after very little internal debate cycled into town with the intention of going to the cinema. She really couldn't go to the Young Farmers' dance alone – it would be too obvious – and there didn't seem to be much else to do. The fairground was doing good trade, but Joe had been right about it being a little rough. She could see, even as she rode past, several youths slouching on the fringes of the lighted booths with their hands in their pockets and their eyes cocked for opportunity.

The film she chose was interesting enough, and while she was absorbed in the action she forgot that she was here alone, and quite enjoyed herself. When the lights went up, however, she felt awkward. She looked around and saw several other people sitting on their own. Of course, there must always be people sitting alone in cinemas, she had simply never noticed them before. How sad to be a person who always goes out alone. It was enough to *make* you eccentric.

When the film ended she saw that it was still quite early. I can't go home yet, she thought with dismay. How difficult it must be to live a double life, a life of deception and secrecy. Where could she go? At this time of night she couldn't go to a pub alone, and the cafés that sold coffee without a meal were closed. She was on the brink of giving up and going home to tell Dad the truth, when the memory of her own words came to her:

'There's the discotheque at the Castle Hotel.'

Of course, the very place. On Saturdays there

was no charge to go in, and it was dark enough in there and noisy enough for her to pass unnoticed. She could buy herself a drink and sit over it for a while and then go home. Or, if she met up with Wendy, she could have a little company before ending her evening in a lone cycle ride.

The discotheque was crowded, even more so than usual, because of its being a holiday weekend, she supposed, and she slipped in among the press of bodies without so much as a raised eyebrow, for which she was grateful. It was almost more like a night-club than a disco, with the muted lights and the little tables in alcoves and the spotlighted dancing area. It was quite a smart place, and they often had live acts on in the evenings instead of records: on those occasions there was a charge to come in, and waiter service only at the tables.

After a fairly long wait, Anne managed to secure herself a drink, and she took it and backed out of the crush round the bar and looked for a seat somewhere out of the way where she could listen and watch in peace. She had seen no one yet whom she recognised, so she supposed that there were a lot of holidaymakers here, or perhaps a crowd from one of the nearby towns.

She was pondering on this when a voice at her elbow said.

'Well met by moonlight! Or perhaps I should say, spotlight.' It was Mr Conrad standing beside her, alone, with a glass in his hand. 'So you didn't go to the Farmers' Ball after all?'

'As you see,' Anne said. 'And neither did you.'

'Well I just had a feeling you'd be here tonight,

and so you are. But do my beady old eyes deceive me, or are you all alone and palely loitering, as the poet says?'

'Which poet?' Anne asked, intrigued. He smiled with a charming frankness.

'Well, do you know, I really don't know. I suppose it's the height of bad manners, to quote without knowing who you're quoting.'

'Whom,' Anne corrected him.

'Whom,' he agreed. 'Goats and grammar – what a lot you know!' He put his head a little on one side, surveying her acutely. 'But I was right after all about the having words part. I hope he didn't storm off and leave you here?'

'No, no, I came alone,' Anne said hastily. 'But what about you, are you alone?'

'More or less,' he said, glancing over his shoulder. 'Nothing to speak of. Can I get you a drink?'

'No thanks. I ought to be going, actually,' Anne said automatically. He clapped his hand to his forehead.

'Snubbed again! You really do make the going hard, don't you?'

'I—' Anne began, confused, then, 'you more or less indicated you had someone with you.'

He smiled at her, and it seemed, for all she told herself otherwise, a very special smile, a friendly smile, for her alone.

'No, you misunderstood me. I was chatting to a girl over at the bar when I saw you come in, but neither of us had any great expectations of the other. Look, have you really got to go, or were you just trying to get rid of me?'

72

His frankness appealed to her, for it seemed the sort of thing one might say to a friend. It would be nice to have someone to talk to like that. She shook her head.

'No, I really do have to go, you see—'

'Then let me give you a lift home,' he said eagerly, interrupting her.

'I have a bicycle,' she said, which was what she had been about to explain.

'Well you could leave that here. You have a padlock, I'm sure.'

'But then I'd have to come in on the bus to collect it. It would be very inconvenint. No, I really have to go, and on the bike.'

He looked distressed. 'I don't like to let you go like that, when I've a perfectly good car waiting outside. But, as you say . . .' He thought for a moment and then shrugged. 'Let this be a lesson to me to get a roof-rack for my car. Then I could have taken the bike too.'

'Or,' added Anne, her sense of humour uppermost again, 'to buy a bike, then you could have escorted me home.'

He laughed. 'I think I'll stick to four wheels. I don't think I'd stand much chance on two.'

Chance of what? Anne wondered as she cycled quickly home through the dark lanes.

Five

'Did you and Joe have a quarrel?' Dad asked Anne the next morning at breakfast.

'No, why?' Anne asked, her heart sinking. She already knew the answer.

'Well, he came round last night to see you. I thought you'd gone out with him. I was quite worried, until I thought you must have quarrelled, and you'd gone out without him in a huff.'

'We didn't quarrel,' Anne said. 'It was just – well, I don't know how to say it – a momentary coldness between us, I suppose. What did he say?'

'Oh, nothing much. You know Joe. I said you'd gone out and he said, oh, and then he said he'd come round today to see you.'

'Did he say when?' Anne asked, trying to sound unconcerned.

'No, but I expect it'd be after dinner. Where did you go, then?'

'Last night? Oh, to the pictures, and then I dropped in at the Castle for a while.'

'On your own? You're a funny girl,' Dad said. 'Why didn't you tell me about you and Joe?'

'There was nothing to tell, really,' Anne said. 'And I didn't want to upset you. I know how fond you are of Joe.'

'Well I am, but I thought you were too.'

'I am, but—'

'But what?'

'Oh, I don't know Dad. I really don't.' She tried to change the subject. 'Are you going for a spin on your bike later?'

'I might do,' he said, and cocked an eye at her. 'You want to be on your own with Joe, is that it?'

'Oh no, I didn't mean that,' she said hastily, but Dad only smiled.

'Don't you worry, I'm not offended. I know what it was like when I was courting your mother: time alone was a precious thing, hard to get.'

'But I didn't mean . . .'

'Don't you mind,' Dad said. 'I want to get out for a bit anyway. Might get some dandelions. Thought of making some dandelion wine this year. I'll pop out for a spin after dinner.'

Dinner was over and cleared away, and Dad had gone before Joe arrived.

'I had one or two things to do up Haldane's, so I couldn't get away sooner,' he said as Anne let him in. He seemed the same Joe as always, except perhaps a little more solemn.

'That's all right, Joe. Dad's gone out for a bit on his bike. Would you like a cup of tea?'

'Wouldn't say no,' Joe said. Normally he would have followed her into the kitchen and chatted to her while she made it, but this time he stayed where he was put, formally, in the sitting room, and Anne's heart sank as she waited for the kettle to boil. It seemed to bode ill, though quite what she was afraid of she couldn't be sure.

She brought in the tea things and biscuits on a tray, and Joe jumped to his feet as soon as she appeared in the doorway and took the tray from her, all attentive good manners. It reminded her of the very first evening, when he had brought her a box of chocolates, though to be fair, his manners had always been perfect towards her. He had never failed in that.

She sat down and poured the tea, and felt the constrained silence that was building up between them. For the first time in years she felt ill at ease with him, as if they were strangers to each other. Well, in a way, perhaps they were. How much of what Joe thought had she ever known? She remembered how, fleetingly, last night she had felt more at ease with a man whose first name she didn't even know, than she did now with Joe, whom she had known for four years.

'I came round to see you last night,' he began after a while.

'Yes, Dad told me. I was out.' That was a silly thing to say, of course he knew she was out. He didn't say anything, and she thought perhaps he was angry. He had his head down, staring at the pattern on the carpet between his feet. 'I went to the pictures,' she said. He still didn't reply. 'I didn't know you were coming round.' she said reasonably. 'You didn't say anything on Thursday when you left me, and you didn't phone or call, so I couldn't be expected to know you were coming round, could I?' She was trying not to sound peeved, and he lifted his head at last and regarded her with his wide blue eyes.

'Oh, that's all right, you don't have to explain to me,' he said. She misunderstood, thinking he was speaking ironically, and began to justify herself again, but he broke in.

'No, no, I quite understand. It was my fault for not ringing you up. It slipped my mind that I hadn't said anything about it on Thursday.'

She saw suddenly that he was being quite genuine in taking the blame to himself. He really was not resentful that she had gone out. She saw, too, that in normal circumstances she would have assumed that he would be calling round for her, even if he did not phone. It was the fact that she thought they had quarrelled that had made her think he would not come. She felt confused and ashamed, but at the same time, piqued. Did she really know so little about him after all this time that she could not judge his reactions to any given situation?

He sat, quiet and calm, as relaxed and alert as a great golden lion. He held his teacup in one strong hand, and seemed to dwarf the room, the furniture, even the house, with his image of strength, as if he were some wild animal who had consented of his free will to be shut up in this cage with her. Anne wondered at how strange he seemed to her suddenly, though he was as familiar as her own heartbeat. She watched him, fascinated.

'I've been doing a lot of thinking, Anne,' he said at last. As he spoke, she realised how rarely he used her name. 'Those remarks you made on Thursday didn't go unnoticed.'

'Joe, I—'

'No, no. I know I'm slow of speech, but I notice things, and I think about them.' He grinned

77

infectiously at her. 'May take me a lot longer than you, but I get there in the end. Anyway, as I said, I've been doing a lot of thinking about the things you said.'

'What things?' she asked faintly.

'Well, about spending money, and splashing out, and treats and so on. I've been saving hard, as you know, and I've not had much money to throw around. But there's justice in what you said, too. There's a time to spend and a time to save. And I knew what you were getting at.'

'Did you?' Anne asked, more faintly still. She hadn't an idea of what he was talking about.

'Of course, these things don't matter so much to a man as to a woman. I don't mean to say I don't care about it – don't get me wrong – I do, of course I do. But, you know, to a man, well, to me anyway, it's the show, and what goes on inside means more than the show, do you know what I mean?'

Anne shook her head, wordlessly, but Joe didn't notice, carried away on the rare flood of his eloquence.

'So I came up to town on Saturday,' Joe went on, reaching into his pocket, 'And I got you this. Of course, you can change it if it isn't what you wanted, but I think I know the kind of thing you like.'

It was, unmistakeably, a jeweller's ring box. He held it out to her, and Anne stared, paralysed, unable to make any move or speak any word. When she did not take it, he opened it for her, and held it out again for her to take the contents – a diamond solitaire. An engagement ring.

At last Anne wrenched her fascinated eyes away from it and looked up at Joe.

'But, Joe—' she began. Their eyes met, and he must have seen the distress in hers. His expression altered, the pleasure and expectation draining out of his face to be replaced by bewildered pain. It was what Anne had always dreaded to cause him, and she wanted to reach out to him.

'You don't want it,' he whispered. His hand still held it out to her, as if he had not yet got control of his muscles. She burst out.

'You didn't ask me!'

'I never thought,' he whispered, his eyes still holding hers in fascination.

'That's just it,' she said bitterly. 'You didn't think. The most important question in your life, and you forgot to ask it.'

'I didn't forget,' he said, growing indignant in his turn. 'I just never thought. I just assumed – well, I always thought that was what we went out for.'

'You assumed!'

'Well we've been going out for all these years. Going steady,' he said defensively. 'Naturally I thought . . . well, anyone would, wouldn't they? I always thought in the end we'd get married. That was what we went out for.'

'You never said so.'

'I thought you knew. I thought you knew I loved you. Do you think I'd go out with you for four years if I didn't love you?'

He stared at her, and she saw the new thought as it entered his mind. 'After all,' he said, and

79

his voice had sunk to a whisper again, 'that was why you went out with me, wasn't it?'

She didn't answer. She didn't know what the truth was, and if she did, she didn't think she'd be able to tell him.

'I always thought you loved me,' Joe said.

'But I did!' she cried, unable to bear the thought of her betrayal. 'I do! At least, I'm very fond of you.'

'Fond!' He looked down at his hand still holding out the despised ring, and withdrew it slowly, closing the box as he did. He stared at it as it lay, white on his brown palm, and then closed his fist around it. 'All right, fond, if you like. But you don't want to marry me?'

'I don't want to marry you just yet. I don't want to marry anyone yet,' she temporised in anguish, but Joe shook his head. He was in control of himself again, and his dignity was more heartbreaking than his pain.

'That won't do, Anne. If you wanted to marry me, if you loved me enough to marry me, you'd know. It wouldn't be a matter of *yet*.'

'But you said—'

'Yes, I know, but I always wanted to marry you. I always *wanted* to. It was only that I felt I couldn't support you in the proper fashion until I'd saved up a bit.'

'I always thought you loved your pigs more than me,' Anne said, and at once could have bitten off her tongue. His dignity intensified.

'I'd have thought I deserved better than that,' he said quietly.

'Oh Joe! Please don't be like that! The last

thing in the world I want is to hurt you, you must believe that. I'm very fond of you. I – I love you. In your own words, would I have gone out with you for all those years if I didn't? But I don't want to marry anyone, not yet.'

'I believe you,' he said. 'I don't believe there's anyone else. But when you love someone enough, there won't be any question of *wanting* to wait. You'll know then, you'll know you're in love properly.'

He stood up, and Anne said, foolishly, 'But you haven't finished your tea.'

'I think I'd better go. I wish you all the very best, Anne. I hope you'll find someone soon.'

'But Joe!' Anne cried. 'You don't mean to go altogether?'

'I think so,' he said firmly.

'But I don't want you to go out of my life,' she said. 'Surely we can still be friends? Surely we can still go out together as before, on a friendly basis?'

'No, I don't think so,' he said gravely. 'You see, I don't feel that way about you. A friendly basis wouldn't be enough for me. I'd want a wife. I feel too much for you, Anne, and if you don't feel that way about me, then I think the sooner we forget each other the better.'

She followed him to the door, dazed, hardly believing that he meant it until she saw him climb into the ancient, tatty old van, and realised that it might be the last time she saw it.

'Joe!' she cried out, but he only lifted a hand to her in farewell, and drove away.

All kinds of feeling flooded over her – distress

and guilt at Joe's unhappiness, surprise at the turn events had taken, anger that she should feel guilty, anger that Joe should take such an absolute view of things. She slammed the door to relieve her feelings, and then wandered back into the sitting room. There the sight of the tea-cups still filled with cooling tea made her realise that Joe had gone for ever. She began to wonder what life was going to be like without his sure, comforting presence in the background, and she sat down on the sofa with tears beginning to prickle her eyes.

What would she ever say to Dad? He would accept the facts in wounded silence, he would shake his head sadly when he thought she wasn't looking. Then Joe's face came before her in a flash of memory, and she thought of the ring, the touching, pathetic, rejected ring, thought of him choosing it for her, and now having to take it back with all his hurt pride, and the tears burst through the flood gates and she flung herself down among the cushions, sobbing.

Joe, so kind, so good, always so tender and courteous to her, loving her in his silent way all this time; she had never wanted to hurt him, and now she had hurt him in the worst possible way. And in a purely selfish way she had hurt herself, depriving herself of his company and support. What would she do without him? Her Saturdays would all be as desolate as yesterday from now on.

She had just about got to the end of her tears and was in the process of mopping herself up when she remembered that she had not even told him the good news about the land. She wouldn't be able to tell him now, it would have to be done by letter after all, and it would stir up his unhappiness again, knowing that now she would not be there to share it with him. Anne struggled for a moment, and then abandoned herself, on a once and for all basis, to a good howl.

She had mopped herself up for the second time by the time Dad came home, but her eyes must have been red enough to tell him that something was wrong. However, he took it better than she would have expected.

'Joe gone, love?' he asked as he came in.

'Yes, Dad,' she said, and explained the situation, that Joe asked her to marry him, and that she had refused, and that he had decided it was best to break off once and for all. Dad nodded gravely, but said nothing until she had finished, and then, after looking at her penetratingly for a moment, he had closed the subject and said instead.

'Would you like a cup of tea?' which was his way of offering silent sympathy.

She had expected a miserable weekend, but Monday turned out to be more bearable than she thought, and having had a long walk in the fields and woods nearby and come in hungry as a consequence, and having made a hearty tea, she found herself thinking cheerfully about going back to work the next day.

'All I need,' she thought, 'is something to keep me occupied. It isn't the end of the world by any means. It could, on the contrary, be the start of a whole new life.'

And on that optimistic note, she went to bed.

83

Six

On Monday at lunchtime Anne went up to Castle Street and had lunch with Wendy, at her insistence, in the cafeteria in Woolworths.

'It's the under-manager,' Wendy explained as they took their trays to a table. 'I've discovered that he has his lunch at this time. They rope off a bit of the canteen for the floorwalkers to have their lunch – look, over there.'

Anne looked. 'So he has his lunch. So what?'

'He's gorgeous, that's what,' Wendy said severely.

'Oh Wendy,' Anne said, laughing. 'You're impossible. What about Graham?'

'Oh, Graham!' Wendy made an expressive face. 'He just doesn't understand me.'

'So Graham's out on his ear?'

'Yup.'

'So you say. I'll believe it when it happens.'

Wendy smiled. 'Well, perhaps you're right. Anyway, what about you? Tell me your news.'

Anne told her about breaking up with Joe, and about meeting the dark stranger again.

'And you mean you still don't know his name?' Wendy asked, more impressed with the latter piece of news than the former. In her own chronic state of uncertainty, she could not regard such fluctuations of romance as either serious or permanent.

'Not his first name,' Anne admitted.

'Some friend you are! Why didn't you ask?'

'It didn't occur to me that you were burning to know. Anyway, it seems that he's staying around for a while, so you'll probably get the opportunity to ask for yourself.'

'Not if he's going to your firm for his business,' Wendy said gloomily. 'Why did he have to chose an old-fashioned, one-horse job like your firm when there's a bright, modern, go-ahead place only a few minutes' walk away? He needs his head examining.' Then her face brightened. 'But that's a good opening, when I finally get to meet him! I can try to persuade him to change firms. Unless . . .' Her face fell again.

'Unless what?' Anne asked.

'Unless he chose your firm because you work there. After all,' she went on in spite of Anne's scoffing, 'you seem to meet up with him with suspicious regularity. Are you *sure* you don't know his first name? You wouldn't hold out on me would you?' she pleaded. 'Not on your old friend Wendy?'

'You're crazy,' Anne laughed, 'but I suppose that's the way I like you.'

'Just promise me one thing,' Wendy said, straight-faced. 'That I can be a bridesmaid at your wedding.'

'Not only that,' Anne said, equally serious, 'you can be *bride* at my wedding.'

A moment of silence, and then they both burst out laughing.

Anne had not forgotten the problem of the good news she had not broken to Joe, and having toyed with the idea of telling Mr Cass that she was no longer friendly with Joe and having him write a letter, she decided that there was no need to be *that* unfriendly. It would almost be an insult, and she bore Joe no ill-will – on the contrary, she was still as fond of him as ever. So she rang through to Haldane's Farm, and asked the girl who answered to pass on a message to Joe Halderthay, asking him to ring her when he had a moment. With anyone else, she wouldn't have been able to leave such a message, for anyone else would think she was wanting to rouse up old problems and wouldn't ring.

Joe, however, whatever he thought she wanted to talk about, and however he felt about her, would never be so discourteous as not to ring when she had asked him to. He was that sort of person, and Anne had always known how to value his particular qualities. So she waited confidently for his call.

In the meantime, she was interested to find out the details of Mr Conrad's proposed buy, since the routine part of it came to her to deal with. He was interested in a building and forecourt on the corner of High Street and Beef Lane, a narrow alley that led down to the site of the old Shambles, on the corner of the market place.

The building was a long, low warehouse with living accommodation on top, and the large forecourt held a derelict petrol pump. In the old days, most shops that sold general wares also sold petrol, for actual garages or service stations were confined to the main trunk roads. It was quite common to have two or three grocery-cum-general stores in each village, each with a petrol pump and a paraffin pump outside. The modern trend however was away from this, and the site in question had not sold petrol for some time.

In fact, the site in question had not sold anything for some time. Anne discovered, in the course of her enquiries, that it had been empty for well over a year, the previous owner having gone out of business and having sold the property to cover some of his bad debts. It was owned by a saw-mills who were apparently happy enough to leave it 'fallow' as Joe might say. Anne wondered idly what the dark stranger wanted with the place, idly because of course she was bound to find out in the end. She was in the delightful position of having to do nothing to find out about him and his business – it would all come to her.

He came in on Wednesday, briefly, to give some piece of information or other to Mr Whetlore. Mr Whetlore had not told her this. He always played his hand close to his chest, in the vain and illusory hope that she would remain in the dark. Though it was a flying visit, Mr Conrad still had a pleasant smile and a cheerful word for Anne; he did not regard her, as some of the clients did, as a part of the furniture.

'Hello,' he said. 'How are you?'

'As well as can be expected,' she answered.

'You sound like a hospital bulletin. Are you unwell?'

'Oh no, life just seems a little complicated just now.'

'Nothing serious, I hope?'

'Oh no, nothing serious.'

'Good,' he said.

'You sounded almost as if you meant that,' Anne said. He looked surprised.

'Shouldn't I?' he asked.

'It's generally only politeness.' He smiled at this.

'*Only* politeness! If you knew what a difference politeness makes, you wouldn't call it an "only".'

Anne blushed a little. 'I didn't quite mean that,' she began.

'I'm glad,' he said quickly, 'because if you remember, we promised each other a polite relationship right from the very beginning.'

'So we did,' Anne said, feeling that she was rapidly being outclassed as far as clever remarks went. She was not put to further test, for at that he simply smiled his slightly lopsided smile, and left.

It was late that afternoon that Joe telephoned her – so late that she was in the process of clearing up to go home.

'Oh, I'm glad I caught you,' Joe said, sounding a little breathless. 'I'm sorry I left it so late, but we've had a busy day, and I couldn't get to the phone sooner.'

'That's all right, Joe,' Anne said soothingly. 'I knew you'd phone.'

'What's the problem?' he asked, sounding a little anxious.

'No problem; rather the reverse. It's just that I had some good news for you which I meant to give you over the weekend, but, what with

88

various events, I forgot to pass it on. It's about the land you're interested in.'

'Oh,' Joe said, and there were many conflicting emotions in that one word. Anne wondered, fleetingly, if he was sorry it hadn't turned out to be on a personal matter that she wanted him to phone.

'I expect you can guess what it is – the news I mean.'

'The land is up for sale?'

'That's right. Apparently they need to raise some cash, and that particular piece is the obvious thing to sell, not being attached to anything else at the moment. Mr Cass says it's up to him whether to sell privately or on the open market, and since you're a customer of his, he's going to give you first refusal.'

There was a long silence, and in the end Anne said, 'Are you still there?'

'Yes, yes, I'm still here. I was thinking.' Another long silence. 'Do you know what the price is?'

'No, he didn't say. I should think it's a matter for discussion between you and Mr Cass. He is a Trustee, after all.'

'That means coming in to see him,' Joe said slowly.

'Yes, of course. But you'd have to anyway, wouldn't you?'

'Yes, but—'

'But what? Surely you can get the time off; you've never had trouble before.'

'It's not that,' Joe said, and added in such a low voice she hardly heard it. 'It's you.'

89

'Oh Joe.' Her heart turned a little in her breast. 'I'm sorry. I never wanted to hurt you, you know that.'

'Yes I know. It wasn't your fault. I suppose I must just get used to the idea.'

Better to stick to business, she thought. 'Well, I'll tell Mr Cass you'll be coming in. No need to make an appointment; he knows how you're fixed and he'll see you any time.'

'Yes, thank you. Tell him I'll try and come in on Monday – better get my word in as quickly as possible.'

There was a glimmer of humour in that speech, and Anne was glad.

'Yes, I think so. I'll see you on Monday, then.'

Joe didn't sound too happy about it, but Anne was pleased at the thought of seeing him again: after all, they had been friends for four years, and she missed him.

Dad, when she got home, was gloomy.

'I've been round to see the place,' he told her by way of greeting.

'What place?' she asked absently, and then the penny dropped. 'Oh, you mean—'

'The bungalow. The *dwelling*, as they call it. I've written to tell them I won't have it. There's always been a resident station master in Winton Parva, since time began. If they don't want to repair this place, they can rebuild it.'

'But Dad, you know they won't,' Anne said.

'They can't put me out,' he said robustly. 'What can they do – throw me out on the street? Drag me out of here by force? This is my home, and yours too, since you won't be marrying Joe. They can't leave us homeless. They'll have to do something.'

'But they have, they've offered you alternative accommodation,' Anne said despairingly. 'They don't have to do anything more about this place. They can let it fall down around our ears. They've nothing to reproach themselves for, if they've offered us another place that's reasonable.'

'Reasonable! What's reasonable about a bungalow miles from the station, a modern bungalow at that, a thing like a cheese-dish on a concrete table!'

'Is it really that bad, Dad?' she asked gently. He turned on her, amazed.

'Are you on their side? Don't you care anything about your own home?'

'Of course I care, but I don't see there's anything that we can do.'

'Well you ought to know what we can do: you're the one who knows all about buildings and property and such-like.'

'That's exactly it, Dad. I'm not a qualified surveyor, but even I know that this place needs a lot of work done on it. The foundations are sinking, and there's no mains sewage. Why should they spend money rebuilding this house when they've others ready for us just to move in?'

'If you don't know that, my girl, then you don't deserve to live in a house like this.'

'Oh Dad, I don't mean that, and you know I don't. All I'm saying is that they won't see it that way. They'll only see the money side of it. But we'll stick it out, and fight, if that's what you want.'

'It's what I want, and it's what I'll do. If my little girl's staying here with me, I'm going to make sure she has a proper home, and the place she's known all her life.' He stumped over to the sink to fill the kettle. 'Blooming mousetrap!' he muttered under his breath. Anne smiled fondly at his back.

'There was some good news today, Dad,' she said to cheer him up. 'Mr Cass told me that the piece of land Joe's interested in has come up for sale and he's giving Joe first refusal, so I phoned him up today to tell him.'

'Well, that's nice. I expect he was pleased.'

'Pleased about the land,' she said. 'He didn't seem so pleased that he would have to come into the office on Monday to see Mr Cass about it.'

'Oh, he's coming in to the office, is he?' Dad said, nodding significantly. 'Well well.'

'Now Dad . . .'

'You never know, Anne my girl, you never know. Great oaks from little acorns grow.'

'Joe's no acorn,' Anne said.

Anne was determined not to spend Thursday alone, and she went across to the café to meet Wendy with the firm intention of securing her company that afternoon and, if possible, evening. Even if Wendy had already arranged to go out with Graham, they might agree to take her along with them as far as the door, so that she would at least have the opportunity of meeting some new people.

Not, she thought, that there were all that many new people flying around in a town the size of

Winton. You couldn't count the holidaymakers, of course, for they were here today and gone tomorrow. And her thoughts returned, inevitably, to the one stranger who was apparently staying put for the time being.

Wendy, too, asked about him when they had settled down with their coffee.

'Have you seen anything of him? I wonder if he'll come in for coffee again?'

'I should think he'll be too busy with his business enquiries,' Anne said. 'Anyway, never mind him now, I want to ask you something.'

'No I can't lend you any money.'

'Oh hush! Can I meet you at the market this afternoon?'

'Of course, if you like. I don't mind wandering round the old place. Joe working?'

'Oh Wendy, I *told* you Joe and I were finished! Don't you ever listen?'

'Of course I do, I just don't take it in. Now you come to mention it, I do recall you saying something about it, but of course I took no notice. After all you and Joe are like Victoria and Albert – practically a National Institution. Is it really serious?'

'I'm afraid so.'

'Afraid? You mind, then?'

'Of course I mind,' Anne said indignantly. 'I'm very fond of Joe. It wasn't my idea to break it off. I'd have been happy enough to go on seeing him, as a friend. But Joe didn't want that.'

'All or nothing, eh? Well, I suppose I can understand that. We passionate types are like that, but it would be hard to understand for a cold, efficient person like you, Anne, all brains and schedules.'

Anne stared at her friend in open-mouthed astonishment as she burbled on.

'You see, there are some people in this life who live on their emotions – warm, loving, exciting people, passionate and temperamental, who need excitement and danger, and live life to the hilt. Whereas people like you – no no! Pax! You don't want to throw that at me, and waste all that lovely cream!' Anne put down the plate she had picked up, and Wendy pretended to wipe her brow. 'Thought I'd had it that time.'

'Passionate and temperamental – you!' Anne snorted derisively.

'It reminds me of a story, though,' Wendy said, grinning impishly. 'Could almost be you and Joe. There was a girl, you see, a nice warm-hearted girl, who went out with a farm hand, as it might be Joe . . .'

'Go on, but be careful,' Anne said.

'No, you'll like this,' Wendy said. 'Well, this chap loved her all right, but he wasn't much of a talker, and when he did finally get round to saying something, it was pretty dull talk, about tractors and football, while all she wanted was for him to say how pretty she was, and how much he loved her.

'Well, one afternoon they'd gone for a walk by the river, and they sat down under some trees, and it was all very romantic, but he didn't so much as put an arm round her, let alone whisper sweet nothings in her ear. At last the girl got tired of it, and said to him, plaintively, "Oh Jack, whoi don't you say someth'n soft?"

'And he thought for a long minute, and then said, "Roice – pudden".'

Anne had not long been back from lunch when the outer door opened and Mr Conrad came in, pausing in front of her desk to give her a flourishing bow.

'Madam, your servant,' he said.

'Pleased to have you know me,' Anne replied grandly. She was not going to be outdone today. He smiled crookedly.

'What a blessing it is to have plenty of excuses to come in here.'

'What's today's excuse?' she asked, not rising to the bait.

'Something I forgot to say last time I came. I always make it a point to leave something unsaid, just in case I want to come back. How's life treating you?' he asked, suddenly serious. 'You don't look as cheerful as you used to.'

'I'm sure I do,' Anne said indignantly. 'I should never let my personal life interfere with my work.'

'Great resolve. But that means there's something wrong with your personal life?'

'Mr Conrad, you take liberties,' she fenced.

'Michael,' he said. 'Michael F. Conrad. I would be honoured if you'd call me Michael.'

'What's the F. for?' she asked, full of curiosity. Now at last she'd be able to satisfy Wendy's curiosity.

'I don't like my second name. I never tell anyone what it is.'

Anne laughed. 'You won't be able to keep it from me. It's one of the pieces of information we have to have from you, and I'm the keeper of the files. So I shall know sooner or later.'

'Cruel woman! You'll be party to all my dark secrets, and hold them over me, and bend me to your wicked will!'

'Don't you ever stop fooling?' she asked him, laughing. His face straightened.

'Sometimes. The F is for Frederick, and if you laugh at me I shall never speak to you again.'

She was serious in her turn. 'I should never laugh at you. And I think Frederick is a beautiful name.'

'Thank you. Do you like cars?'

Anne blinked at the sudden change of subject. 'Some cars,' she said warily, thinking of Joe's scrap-heap van.

'What kind of car do you like best?'

'I don't really know much about them. But I remember once seeing a lovely sports car, a Triumph it was, I know that, but I'm not sure what it would be called.'

'What colour?'

'What colour? Oh, I think it was green. Dark green. Why?'

'No reason.' He jumped up from the edge of the desk on which he was perched. 'I must be going.'

'But don't you want to see Mr Whetlore?'

'Not a lot.' He was at the door. Anne called after him, puzzled.

'But I thought you had business?'

'It'll keep.' His voice floated back over his shoulder, and he was gone.

96

'Strange man,' Anne said to herself, shrugged, and dismissed him from her thoughts.

At two o'clock she was just putting the cover on her typewriter ready to leave when Michael Conrad came back into the office with a breezy smile.

'Miss Symons,' he said, 'your carriage awaits you.'

'Carriage? What are you talking about?'

'I've come to take you away.'

'How did you know I finished at this time?'

'Silly! I've been watching you for a week. I know your routine inside out now. You're a creature of habit, aren't you? Which makes it easier, of course. Anyway, if you're ready, we'll just step outside, onto the magic carpet, and away.'

'I thought you said it was a carriage? Anyway, I can't go anywhere, I have to meet my friend.'

'Nonsense.'

'I have to! It's all arranged.'

'Miss Symons, I have to speak to you very seriously,' he said gravely. 'You really must get rid of this terrible negative attitude you have. You have done your best from the beginning to put me off, but I've persevered. You must learn to say yes to life, Miss Symons, to Life with the big L. Your friend won't miss you. Your personalised jet plane is out in the street, waiting to whisk you away towards the sun. Come.'

Bemused, Anne followed him out and down the stairs into the street where, parked opposite the door against the kerb was a dark green sports car of the sort she had mentioned before. Her jaw dropped inelegantly with surprise, and then she turned speechlessly towards him. He smiled with faint pride.

'I got it right, then? It's a TR5 – remember that, you ignoramus – and the colour, for your further information, is known as British Racing Green. Like it?'

'It's *gorgeous*,' Anne said with feeling. 'But—'

'No buts,' he warned her. 'You've more buts than the goats you know so much about. I'm taking you for a lovely drive in the countryside, and maybe to tea somewhere. That sounds very polite and proper doesn't it? And you'll enjoy it, so jump in, and shut up.

'I don't know whether you're being polite or rude – you have me all confused,' Anne said.

'Good,' he said, helping her in. 'It may help to stop you arguing.'

'But I really did have an arrangement to meet my friend.'

'The little snub-nosed girl? It's all right, I saw her ten minutes ago on the arm of a man who certainly wouldn't thank you for joining them. She won't miss you.'

I suppose that must be Graham, back "on" again, Anne thought. Michael Conrad went round the other side of the car and climbed into the driving seat.

'Ready?' he asked.

'If you're sure.'

'I'm sure. Say "yes" just for once, Miss Symons. You'll find it quite painless.'

'Yes,' Anne said, and the car roared away down the street.

Seven

'I'm going to drive fast now,' he said as soon as they got onto the main road, 'and I like to concentrate when I drive fast, so I won't be talking to you for a while. You can talk if you like, or sing – I shan't mind. You don't mind driving fast?'

'I don't know. I haven't done it much.'

'I'm quite safe. I'm a very good driver. Just sit tight and enjoy it.'

Then he was off. The car, being low to the ground, seemed to travel much faster than it really did, as Anne judged from glances at the speedometer. It was very exhilarating, especially as the hood was down and the wind was rushing around her head. She hunched a little further down in her seat to get the shelter of the windscreen, and, as she had been instructed, enjoyed it.

The car made a pleasant noise, not harsh, but warm and throaty, and he drove so smoothly that she was never jerked or thrown about in her seat. He really is a good driver, she thought, he isn't just boasting – though he hadn't said it boastfully, but as if it were simple fact. When she was not looking at the scenery whisking past her, she took sidelong glances at him, glances that grew longer as she found that he took no notice of her. He really did concentrate, and it gave her the opportunity to study him.

He sat well back in his seat, so that his arms were straight out in front of him, holding the wheel like a racing driver would, and his long legs were stretched forward too. It looked a very comfortable way to drive, and it made her feel safer. He seemed relaxed, and alert at the same time, his eyes on the road, flicking up to the rear-view mirror from time to time. his hands steady on the wheel, or reaching surely for the short, leather-topped gearstick beside him. He had nice hands, she thought, long-fingered, strong hands, as strong as Joe's but more sensitive. Or perhaps sensitive wasn't the right word. Joe's hands were sensitive enough when they were feeling a pig's udder or helping her farrow, but they didn't look as if they might play a violin or paint a picture. Or drive a car.

Michael Conrad really did look the part, from his slightly ruffled dark hair and firm relaxed profile to his elegantly casual clothes – slacks and hacking jacket and a beautiful cream linen open-necked shirt. And his shirt was designed to be open-necked, not like Joe's off-duty wear. He really looked like the kind of person who would drive a – what did he call it? – TR5. It sounded well. I went for a drive in his TR5. She could make a song out of that.

And then, as she thought of the car, the question that hadn't occurred to her since they left the office came back full force: where had he got the car from? Was it the wildest coincidence that he happened to be the owner of the very kind and colour of car she had named? Unlikely. Very unlikely. And yet, what was the alternative? What was he that he could go out and at three hours' notice produce a car to order like that? Where did he get it from? It evidently wasn't a new car, but the inside of it was band-box clean, as if it had just come from a car showroom.

A horrible thought crossed her mind, that perhaps he had stolen it, but she shook the thought away as even more improbable than that he had already owned it. People like him didn't steal cars, and if they did they didn't drive them as relaxedly as he drove this one. He must either have bought it or hired it, but the implications of that were as hard to swallow. Why had he done it? Simply to please or impress her? What kind of interest in her did that imply? She detached her gaze from the floor and looked again at his face, as if it would tell her something.

From this side of his face, his nose looked straight, rather noble, in fact, and his lips in profile, lightly closed, were deep-cut enough to balance out his chin. His eyes were steady and grey under dark brows – an interesting contrast – and his eyelashes were short and dark and spiky, rather like Joe's when he had been in the water. Anne liked his profile, it gave her confidence. She liked his clean-cut jawline, too, and the proud set of his head. He looked as though he would like his own way, and know how to get it. Well, she knew that anyway: he had handled her masterfully enough. Say yes to life, Miss Symons! She laughed at that, and he glanced quickly at her, and at once slowed the car from sixty to thirty and turned off onto the next sideroad on the left.

'Are you happy?' he asked, breaking their long silence.

'Yes,' she said. 'Where are we going?'

'To a place where we can stop at the top of a hill and get a view. It's no good stopping anywhere else, the hedges are all too high to see over. And we have to have a view.'

'Why?'

'To give us a reason for being there, of course.'

'Do we need a reason, Mr Conrad?' Anne asked.

'Now that's an improvement, that remark. But I asked you to call me Michael.'

'But I can't call you Michael if you call me Miss Symons.'

'You've never asked me to call you anything else. I thought the omission was deliberate.'

'You didn't,' Anne said, and he smiled slightly.

'Thanks,' he said enigmatically.

'Anyway, if you need a formal invitation, would you please call me Anne.'

'Delighted.' The car was idling along at thirty-five now, and Michael had leisure to glance at her now and then. 'You had plenty of time to study me – what did you decide?'

'Decide?'

'Have you got me taped? Set me down, all parts neatly labelled, for filing later? Or were you just admiring my profile?'

'Really, you do ask impossible questions!' Anne laughed, not offended.

'You don't seem to find me beyond hope anyway – you haven't screamed to be let out. Well, later I shall have my chance to study you at length, when we've found somewhere to park. That's another reason for finding a view – so that I can study you while appearing to be gazing out of the window at the downs.'

'You don't need to pretend; you're welcome to look at me all you want.'

'Definitely an improvement,' he nodded happily. 'It seems to come over you as we drive away from Market Winton. Shall I tell you what I think, Miss – Anne, I should say? I think that you are playing a part in Market Winton, and playing it so well you are almost deceiving yourself.'

'What part? How deceiving myself?'

'You're not naturally a strict, efficient, habit-bound creature at all. It's all an act. You're wild and free, an adventurer, a creature of impulse who loves excitement and change. And because you have to keep that dull old job in the solicitors' office, you've locked that wild person away inside a cold efficient person who says "no" and "why" to everything. But you're still there inside, like a fly in amber, only so far inside you've forgotten what you're really like.'

'Now how can you work all that out from the little you've seen of me?' Anne asked, fascinated.

'Oh,' he said airily, 'that's nothing. I can do things you've never even imagined before.'

'I'm sure,' she said dryly. 'In fact, I know nothing at all about you. Except your name.'

'Not to worry, we've the whole afternoon in front of us – time enough to find out everything.'

'Everything? In one afternoon?'

'I don't see why not. After all, we don't want to drag it out, do we? We can find out the important things in that time.'

'What do you consider the important things?' Anne asked, thinking of what he was doing in Winton, where he came from, what he did for a living.

'Oh, what sort of music you like best, and what are your favourite wines, and do you prefer French food to Italian – that sort of thing.'

'I never know if you're serious, or joking,' Anne complained. He smiled at her, turning his head so that she could see the smile's lopsidedness.

'That's part of my charm.'

It is, said Anne, but only to herself.

He stopped the car at last near the top of a hill, pulling it into a gateway so that it would be out of the way of any traffic passing. 'We have to walk a little way from here,' he said.

'Do you know this part of the world, then?' she asked in surprise. She had always imagined that he was a stranger to Dorset.

'No, I've never been here before.'

'Then . . .?'

'My dear girl, we have to get to the top of that ridge in order to get the view we need, and it's obvious that the road goes downhill from here. So we climb over the gate and walk up there through that field to where those trees break the skyline, and we should find some-where pleasant enough to sit and continue our mutual inquisition.'

'Not *over* that field,' she said, happy to have found something on which to correct him. 'Round it, perhaps. The farmer wouldn't thank you for trampling down his young wheat.'

'But naturally,' he said, smiling with his greatest charm, 'I meant *round* it.'

Under the trees they found a dry knoll on which they could sit with their backs to the trunks and their feet stretched out into the sunshine. The view was magnificent, over a stretch of patch-work countryside that rolled down into a wide valley and up again to the ridge that separated the land from the sea. The cloudless sky took over there, pale blue at the horizon, deepening towards the zenith, rich with the afternoon sunshine.

'Breathtaking,' Michael said after a while spent in silence contemplation of the scene. 'No matter where I go in the world, it's always England I want to come back to. There's no more beautiful country in the world.'

'And there's no more beautiful county than Dorset,' Anne said loyally. He smiled at her but said nothing. 'Have you been abroad much?' she asked.

'I should think,' he said gravely, 'that I've been practically everywhere. How about you?'

'Only to Switzerland, on school journey, and on a day-trip to France,' she admitted, adding brazenly, 'on the Hovercraft from Weymouth, actually.'

He didn't laugh at her. He nodded and said, 'Pity. You've missed a lot. But there's always time to rectify that.'

'It isn't that I didn't want to,' she said quickly. 'But my mother was ill for a long time, so we never really went away at all.'

'You'd like to go abroad?'

'I'd love to travel. It's one of my dreams, but I'm afraid it will probably have to remain a dream.'

'Why?'

'Well, I couldn't afford to travel widely in style, and I'd be too scared to tramp the world alone. I know some people do it, but I haven't that kind of courage.'

'Sleeping under hedges and hitching across the desert and that kind of thing?' Michael asked, amused.

'That kind of thing,' Anne agreed. 'Where have you visited?'

'As I said, almost everywhere.'

'Name one place,' Anne demanded.

'The Mojave desert,' he said, apparently at random.

'I don't even know where that is,' she admitted.

'I'm glad of that,' he said, grinning. 'What an ignorant girl you are!'

'I'm not an ignorant girl – I know about goats. And conveyances.' Their eyes met. 'Which reminds me—'

'I knew you'd get round to it,' he said.

'What do you want to buy that place in the High Street for? What kind of business are you setting up?'

'That's two, you're allowed one more.'

'One more what?' Anne was puzzled.

'Question. I thought it would come to this. You're a terrible girl for asking questions.'

'It's part of my charm, to quote someone.'

'One more,' he insisted.

'What do you do for a living?'

'That's practically the same as the other two. You don't show much originality.'

'You haven't answered them yet,' she reminded him. 'You can expand as much as you like on the answers.'

'It's a dull subject to be talking about while we're sitting here in this lovely sunshine with this lovely view to look at.'

'Answer!'

'All right. I'm opening a garage. I'm going to buy old cars and sell them again at a profit. I'm in the second-hand car business. Happy now?'

Anne was thinking. 'Of course, that accounts for—'

'Everything,' he finished for her.

'The car,' she corrected. 'I've racked my brains to work out how you got hold of that car at such short notice.'

He seemed amused. 'And you think you have the answer now? You know exactly how I did it?'

'I – well, not exactly *how* – but . . .'

'I'll tell you, and put you out of your misery. I telephoned through to a contact of mine in Weymouth who deals in Triumph cars. He had this one in his showroom, and he got a lad to drive it up straight away. I must admit the colour was a piece of pure luck, but otherwise, it was quite straightforward.'

'It's a lovely car,' she said. 'And now I know how, but I still don't know why.'

'Why I got it? Oh, I think you can work that one out for yourself,' Michael said, smiling into her eyes. Anne felt her face grow warm, and he turned his head away to look at the view with a complacent smile.

The silence extended itself in the drowsy afternoon and they both sat quietly, happy just to enjoy the peace of their surroundings. The sunlight lay rich and golden like butter across the fields, throwing longer shadows from the hedges and trees as the afternoon crept on. The swallows were busy in the insect-laden air, and their squeaking and the occasional burring buzz of a bee in the clover were the only sounds that reached them.

Anne looked at her companion, and saw that he, like her, was quite relaxed and completely happy, gazing away into the blue distances with a serene smile on his lips. She was on the other side of him now, and was looking at his other profile, the crooked side of his face. It was astonishing that the two sides of the same face could look so different. His other profile had been that of a man of action and determination, a businessman, capable and firm. This profile was that of a dreamer, somehow gentler, vaguer. His crooked nose and lopsided, curly mouth were somehow less inaccessible, their imperfections more lovable than his other profile's elegance. The firm, determined man of action might sweep her off her feet, but the gentle dreamer would be the one who would keep her.

A second-hand car business, she mused. It was not a thing she could have guessed, but it explained the slightly too slick air there was about him when he was involved in his business dealing. She had the impression from somewhere that the used-car business was run almost exclusively by crooks, and it troubled her a little that he should be involved in it. Not that she believed for a moment that there was anything crooked about him – he was obviously honest – but she felt if she mentioned to anyone, like her father, that this was his line of business, they might think the worse of him.

And why, she asked herself suddenly, should it matter to you what other people think of him? And yet, here she was, sitting in a field with him miles from anywhere just as if she had known him all her life. Strange how close she felt to him, though she had known him only a few days; closer than she had felt to Joe after four years.

'What were you thinking about?' she heard his voice breaking into her thoughts, and coming to, she realised that he had been studying her for some time as she stared into space.

'Oh, all kinds of things,' she said. 'Cars and my father and . . .' she hesitated to say it.

'And?'

'You.'

'That's good. I was thinking about you.

Wondering what you've done with your life all these years, tucked away here in this quiet grey town in the middle of the green bit of England. Wondering what you did for excitement, how you managed to hold down that wild part of yourself without going mad in the process.'

'It hasn't seemed too hard, really,' she admitted.

'I'd go completely potty if I were to stay in the same place for longer than – the merest fraction of a hesitation – 'a year.'

'I suppose it's self-discipline,' she said. 'I don't allow myself to get bored. Whatever I'm doing, I concentrate on it, make it interesting. And I don't sit around in my spare time: I'm always doing. So I get by.'

'I admire you for it,' Michael said seriously. 'I really admire you.' She turned to meet his eyes. He seemed to mean more than he said.

'Do you?' she asked. His curly mouth was very close to hers, his candid grey eyes held her in their gaze. She found it hard to remember the swallows wheeling in the sunlight and the whisper of the wind in the leaves; hard to remember the world at all. All the passion of her nature which had been suppressed, which had never before had an object worthy of it, was pouring upwards in her, threatening to carry her away in a flood of sweetness – madness. His long-fingered hand lifted hers from the grass and curled around it, warm and strong.

'Yes, I do. I admired you from the first moment I saw you. I felt you were like a caged tiger.'

Remember, she told herself desperately, this is the man who just a moment ago told you he

110

could not bear to stay in the same place for long. He's just passing through. He caressed her hand, and the world was receeding farther and farther away. Not passing through, her mind whispered. He's staying, for a while. He lifted her hand to his lips and kissed it, and then gave it back to her, and, released, she felt she must fall from the dizziness of this new emotion.

'It must be getting late,' she heard herself saying. 'Look how long the shadows are.'

'Yes,' Michael said briskly, 'and you're getting cold sitting in the shade here. Look how goosey your arms are. Come on, let's go and have some tea somewhere.'

He jumped to his feet and held out his hand to help her up, and when she grasped it, the world began to shift back into focus, and it was simply a strong, capable hand heaving her to her feet. Two profiles, two hands, two men. Or was it her nature that had two sides, after all?

'You haven't told me yet anything of great importance – like what books you read, and what music you like, and what your favourite colour is,' he said as they walked briskly down the hill towards the gate.

'I should think you know the answer to that last,' she said, light-spirited again.

'Oh yes, of course, British Racing Green!' He laughed. 'Well, that's a start. We can find out one or two other things on the way to the tea shop.'

'Where are we going? Have you decided?'

'The Copper Kettle. Have you been there?'

'No, never.' It was rather nice, after all these

111

years with Joe, to be with someone who decided the whole thing from beginning to end, and without reference to the price.

'Are you hungry? I should think you must be, not having had any lunch. You looked quite pale back there on the hill – I thought you were going to pass out.'

Anne glanced at him quickly, to see if he really thought it was hunger and not passion that had made her dizzy a moment ago, and she found that he was smiling at her with his most enigmatic expression. She could tell nothing from his face, and he knew it.

'Yes, I'm hungry,' she said at last, non-committally.

'Thought you were,' he said. 'Never mind, fix your mind on hot buttered toast and scones and jam and other good things. We won't be long now.' He climbed the gate with lithe agility and jumped down on the other side. Joe would have undone the gate, patiently, held it for her, and done it up again afterwards. She climbed over, and when she got to the top, Michael turned back and held up his arms to her, to help her down.

She opened her mouth to say 'I can manage, thank you,' and then shut it again. Why deny him the opportunity? His strong hands closed on her waist, she leaned down and put her arms round his neck, and he lifted her carefully down. For a long moment after her feet had touched the ground he kept hold of her, looking down into her eyes and smiling, and then, almost as if he had said to himself, it is not yet time, he released her gently and they walked towards the car.

They had a pleasant and leisurely tea in the Copper Kettle and discussed such neutral topics as books, music and food. When Michael had called for the bill, he leaned towards her across the table and said.

'What shall we do tonight?'

'Tonight? I hadn't thought. I—'

'You what? Now don't tell me you've made arrangements already.'

'Only with Wendy,' she said guiltily. 'I didn't want to spend tonight on my own, and she and her boyfriend usually go to a dance or something like that, so I arranged to go with them.'

'That's all right, then,' he said with feigned relief. 'I thought for a moment you were going to tell me you'd already got a date.'

'I haven't yet said I'd go anywhere with you, though,' she said. He raised one eyebrow coolly.

'You haven't any choice. You don't seem to realise, my dear Miss Symons, that you've put yourself completely in my power. Here you are, miles from anywhere, and no way of getting back except with me, in the car. If you don't agree to come out with me tonight, I have the power to leave you stranded here – a sort of hijack in reverse.'

'In that case, Mr Conrad, I shall have, most reluctantly, to agree.'

'Reluctantly – of course.'

'Of course.'

'But don't forget, if you try to change your mind . . .'

'Yes?'

'I have your bike in Market Winton as a hostage.'

'Not my bike!'

'Double-cross me, baby,' he drawled, 'and you'll never see that bike alive again.'

Eight

'And who,' asked Dad in his most old-fashioned voice, 'is Michael Conrad when he's at home?'

Anne paused in the middle of brushing her hair to look at her father in the mirror with an expression of exasperation. Michael had driven her home and had promised to pick her up later in the evening and take her for a drink. Dad had been pleased that she was going out, until he asked her with whom.

'Now Dad, don't look like that. He's a client of Mr Whetlore's, he's buying property in the High Street, and he's perfectly respectable.'

'*I* don't know him,' Dad said stubbornly. 'Where's he live? What's he do? I've never heard of him.'

'Well you wouldn't have. He's new to town. He's staying at the Black Bear, and he's going to start up a business here.'

'What sort o' business?'

'A garage,' Anne said, adding reluctantly, 'and second-hand cars.'

'Ah!' Dad said with a world of significance. 'That's it, then? Well Anne, my lass, I'd 'a thought you'd know better than to mix yourself up with someone in that line of trade.'

'I told you, Dad, he's one of Mr Whetlore's clients.'

'Client or no client, used cars is full of crooks. Plenty of money, I'll bet?'

'He doesn't seem to be short,' Anne began.

'See what I mean? Where's he get all that money from?'

'You seem to think that no honest man could possibly have more than ten bob in his pocket,' Anne said crossly.

'That's as may be,' Dad said, one of his unanswerable phrases with which he bogged down arguments. 'But I'm telling you there's more crooks in used cars—'

'You make it sound like some kind of packaging,' Anne said. Dad frowned at her.

'Don't get smart with me, Miss. I'm telling you for your own good. What do you know about him? Nothing! You don't even know that his name's his name.'

'I—'

'Well?'

'You're right, of course,' Anne said, realising that it was no good losing her temper with her father. 'I only know what he tells me and what I observe for myself. But he's all right. He isn't anything out of the ordinary. And I'm only going out for an evening with him, I'm not going to marry him, you know!'

'There's many a girl has said that, and found out later, when it's too late.'

'Do you think he's going to white-slave me? Honestly Dad,' she began to smile, her sense of humour re-asserting itself, 'you've got this terrible attitude to strangers. Everyone's a stranger somewhere. If you went to London,

116

you'd be a stranger, but it wouldn't change the fact that you're a kind, honest, thoroughly straight man, now would it?'

'You could always wheedle,' Dad said gloomily, allowing Anne's arm to creep round his neck. 'Well, I'll let you go out this once, against my better nature, but tomorrow I'm finding out about this Michael Conrad, and if he isn't all he seems to be—'

'You'll be after him with a shotgun. All right, Dad, I understand. But now I must get ready. I don't want to keep him waiting.'

'You keep any man waiting as long as you want,' Dad said as he went out. 'If he doesn't think you're worth waiting for . . .'

Anne was ready by the time Michael called for her, and went out with him to find, to her surprise, a different car, a bright yellow one that she recognized, despite her ignorance, as a Capri.

'What happened to the other one?' she asked when she had settled herself in the front seat.

'This one's my car,' Michael said, as if it was an explanation. 'I prefer comfort and warmth. And in any case, I wouldn't drive a dark green car at night. Or a dark blue one. Yellow or white – be seen, that's my motto.'

Anne laughed. 'You do sound rich! One car for the daytime and one for the night. I suppose you have a change of car for each suit?'

'You forget, cars are my business,' he said. 'I've always got a wide choice of cars to drive. But in general, for my own use, I'd choose a yellow one. You see, it's been proved that certain colours are more repellent to the eye, and the more repellent, the less likely the car is to be hit.'

'How clever of you to know that,' Anne said. He glanced sideways at her.

'I can never tell if you're trying to tease me or not.'

'That's funny – I said that about you only this afternoon.'

'In that case, we should have a very confused relationship.'

He's repeating himself, Anne thought with disappointment. It was like a tiny questionmark raising its head momentarily in her brain: if he could repeat himself, didn't that prove that he had certain set-pieces which he used on certain occasions?

'Where are we going? she asked suddenly, noticing that they were not driving into town.

'Don't you know?' he asked, grinning derisively. 'I thought you knew this area like the back of your hand.'

'Well of course I know where we *are*,' she said. 'I asked you where we were going. I can see we're heading towards Felsham—'

'We're going to the *"Pure Drop"*.'

'Why?' Anne asked simply.

'Because I've passed it twice in the car, and I thought it was such a beautiful name, I'd have to go there, even if it's only for one quick one. If it's no good we can always drive on somewhere else.'

'What it is to be motorised!' Anne marvelled. The 'Pure Drop' looked like an ordinary, small village pub from the outside, but once inside it was evident that it had recently been taken over. The new owners had converted it and opened up a large room out at the back of the building that had once been a store-room. Anne and Michael eased their way in, for it was quite crowded, and stared around them. There seemed to be an unusual mixture of people, some farm-labourers and local villagers, some well-dressed people from farther out, and some young holiday-makers. The latter were making a particularly noisy group round a bar pool table. There was also a darts game going on on the other side of the room, and someone in another group in a secluded corner had a guitar.

'Not exactly a typical Dorset village pub,' Michael remarked, 'but it doesn't look too bad, Shall we stay for one?'

'Oh yes, if you don't mind it. I quite like the atmosphere,' Anne said.

'All right, then. What will you have?'

Michael left Anne to thread his way through to the bar, having pointed out to her a couple of seats at a table over by the pool-table. Anne had never seen the game played before, though she had played snooker, it being a very popular game at the British Legion where she had often gone with Joe. Anne took the seat with the best view of the table and, as Michael was quite a long time getting the drinks, she had ample opportunity to watch the play and pick up the rudiments of the game.

It was an electrically controlled table which released the balls for a new game when a tenpenny piece was put in the slot. As was customary in pubs, those people who wanted a game had put their coins on the edge of the table, and each came up to claim his turn when his coin was nearest the slot.

Anne watched the last stages of the game that was in progress, and then her view of the table was blocked by some people coming to stand and watch. The cues were laid up, signifying the end of the game, and a new foursome claimed their turn. Anne could only see play intermittently through the bodies that blocked her view, but after a few minutes someone shifted slightly and through the gap she saw that the player lining up his shot was Joe Halderthay.

Anne's first, instinctive reaction, born of four years' habit, was to call his name, to greet him. Then she remembered who she was with, and thought better of it. She stared at him all the same, protected from his casual glance by the fence of bodies between them. This was the man she might have married.

He was stooped over the table in the correct position for a snooker player, sighting along his arm, the cue running along the slight cleft in his chin. He was wearing his usual clean white shirt with the neck open, his skin showing brown against the whiteness. The sleeves were rolled up, and his powerful forearms glittered with a sheen of blonde hairs bleached almost white against the darker tan of his arms.

His face was stern with concentration, his level blue eyes narrowed, his lips slightly parted over his white teeth. Anne looked from that remembered face to his blunt, capable hands, and shivered a little. There was immense power in him, in this great golden man, power coiled down in his body poised for the shot. The cue ran forward like a ram-rod; there was a double click of ivory, and then a general murmur of approval from the onlookers as the ball cannoned down the table, curled like a live thing round the back of the black ball, and neatly potted the purple.

It was a terrific shot. Anne smiled to herself. There was something very attractive about a man doing something well, even when it was as trivial a thing as bar pool.

'Sorry I was so long,' a voice broke into her thoughts. Anne withdrew her eyes guiltily, and smilingly accepted the drink that Michael was holding out to her. 'There was such a crowd up at the bar. It must be pay-day or something – I'm sure it can't be packed like this every night.'

'Market day,' Anne said, remembering the fact herself only then. She kept her eyes on Michael's face, for she did not want him to glance across at the table and see Joe there. 'A lot of these chaps will have come up for the market and they often combine it with their weekly night out.'

'Of course, I forgot,' Michael said, 'you'd know all about the farm-workers' schedule, wouldn't you? You were being taken out by a farm-labourer.'

'Not a labourer,' Anne contradicted him automatically. 'He's a pigman.'

She should have said 'stockman', as she realised as soon as she said it, but it was too late now. Michael stared at her for a moment, and then burst out laughing.

'Oh dear, what an unfortunate expression!' he chortled. 'It calls up lovely images, like something out of *Animal Farm*. 'What do you want to be when you grow up, sonny? 'I want to be a pigman, like my father".'

'All right,' said Anne crossly, 'it isn't that funny. Oh hush up! You might offend someone.' And she glanced towards the pool table, hoping Joe hadn't heard. Michael now begin singing, parodying a Beatle's song: 'I am the pigman, I am the walrus—' and she was getting both cross and nervous.

'Shut up,' she said again. 'It's a perfectly respectable trade. Better than being a used-car salesman, anyway.'

At that, Michael stopped laughing, and stared at her. Anne felt slightly ashamed, but still she glanced towards the pool table, and when she said, 'Let's drink up and go, shall we?' he agreed without a word, helped her into her coat and preceded her to the door to make a path for her through the closely-packed bodies. In silence they walked to the car and got in, and Anne thought to herself that, even if she had offended Michael seriously, at least neither he nor Joe had seen the other, and that was an advantage.

Michael started the car and drove down the road a little way, and then abruptly turned into a side road and drove until he came to a gate by a haystack, where he pulled the car in and stopped. He turned to face her, and his expression in the bright moonlight was gentle and curious.

'Was he there?' he asked without any preamble. She stared back at him, unwilling to answer, but seeing that he knew anyway she nodded reluctantly. 'I meant no offence, you know,' he went on. 'Nothing against him, it was only the word, the name.'

Anne was so surprised at his words that she did not speak for a moment. She had expected him to be offended, angry, even resentful, and he had instead disarmed her with a kind and understanding apology.

'You must have been very fond of him,' Michael said, scrutinising her face. 'I won't ask why you split up, but I can understand why you don't want to bump into him.'

'No, it isn't anything like that,' Anne said hastily. 'We split up because I wouldn't marry him, and—'

'Yes?' She didn't go on. 'Well, why so anxious to avoid him, then?'

'Because – oh, I don't know. I suppose I thought it would upset him to see me out with someone else,' Anne said, and she thought it sounded foolish, even to her.

'I think I'm beginning to get the picture,' Michael said, the beginnings of a smile lurking round his lips. 'He's a nice chap, slow and steady and very fond of you. You like him but wouldn't dream of marrying him. He never realised you were too good for him and was shocked when you turned him down. And now, are you sure you've no lingering pangs? No

123

little seeds of regret that you didn't say yes instead of no?'

Anne felt herself blushing, and was glad that in the moonlight he would not be able to tell. 'I'm sorry we can't be friends any more,' she said. 'I think he went to extremes there.'

'I can understand it. If you really love someone, you don't want second best. I admire him for that anyway – shows courage. But you haven't answered my question.'

'I have,' Anne said, trying to look at him steadily.

'All right,' Michael said after a moment. 'I think I understand.' There was a brief silence during which Anne felt that it was probably her turn to apologise now.

'I'm sorry I snapped at you in the pub,' she said at last. 'Calling you a used-car salesman. I didn't mean it.'

'Funny how you think that's a rude thing to call someone,' he smiled.

'Oh, I suppose one always associates used cars with crookery. My Dad—'

'Yes?'

'Warned me against you,' she admitted. 'Just on the strength of your job. Why did you go in for it, anyway?'

'Oh, I just drifted in, as I suppose most people do. I always loved cars – any engines, really – right from a child. I loved engines the way other people love animals. I was never happy unless I was taking something to pieces or, later, unless I was under a car.

'I passed my test as soon as I was seventeen,

but I could drive long before that. I bought my first old banger for fifteen pounds and did it up. I used to earn money in the evenings and at weekends doing jobs on people's cars in the neighbourhood, and by the time I was eighteen, it seemed only reasonable to get somewhere where I could do it full time.'

'And you went on from there?'

'I went on from there, building up my business, buying old cars, doing them up and selling them again, and doing services and repairs and so on to other cars. Got some more cash together and got a bigger place in another part of town. Did well. And so it went on. I love cars, and I love travelling. So I combine the two, and move around the country starting up new businesses. I'm like a farmer in that respect,' he said.

'How do you mean?' Anne asked, puzzled.

'Making businesses grow where none grew before,' he laughed. He reached out and took her hand, quite naturally, and Anne startled at the touch.

'So you're really quite respectable,' she said, smilingly.

'Did you doubt it?'

'And rich?'

'Mercenary girl! Yes, I suppose by some standards moderately rich.' His other hand was resting on the back of her seat, and now it moved round behind her and rested on her shoulder. 'So you see—' his face was serious now, his eyes intent, looking into hers in a way that made her feel at once dizzy and excited and afraid.

'I see,' she whispered. He bent his head towards

her, and the shadows flowed across it, leaving it in darkness. His arms drew her in towards him, she felt the warmth of him, smelled the spicy scent of him. Her hands went up to his shoulders, though whether to push him away or pull him close she didn't know. His lips touched hers, hesitantly, electrically, and then he was kissing her with passion, his arms around her, and she was responding, her fingers digging into his shoulders to hold him close.

'Anne,' he whispered, releasing her mouth to run his lips over her cheek and ear. 'Beautiful Anne. A caged tiger indeed.'

And she turned her head, seeking his mouth again, not wanting to waste any second of this magical time.

A long while later when they were sitting quietly, her head against his shoulder, he said softly,

'I'm not a pigman, but will I do?'

'Don't tease,' she said. 'I don't want any more talk of pigs or goats or any other members of the farm world.'

'What should it be instead? Carburettors and distributor heads?'

'Certainly,' Anne said firmly. 'I shall learn a whole new language. I shall talk to you in the words of a motor-mechanic. I shall know everything about cars before you can say knife. Or should I say, before you can say gearlever?'

'You funny little thing,' he laughed. 'I don't want you to be a motor mechanic. I want you to be the girl I met in the solicitors' office, the very proper Miss Symons, whose dainty outside conceals a raging tigress.'

'Charming,' Anne laughed. 'The lady who rescued you from the goats.'

'That's right,' he said seriously. 'Don't change.'

And he kissed her again, and even while she clung to him in joy, the small doubts that had been planted were beginning to send up tiny shoots, and something was whispering in her heart, 'Can this really be happening? Can this really be for me?'

For by his own confession, he was a man who liked to travel around, and was it not extremely likely, or almost certain, that he had said the same kinds of things to each new girl in each new town? But it was still only a whisper, and the newly delightful sensation of being kissed by him outweighed it.

Nine

'It's all Graham's fault,' Wendy sighed. 'If it hadn't been for him I might have been going out with Michael Conrad myself.'

'I don't see why it's his fault,' Anne said.

'Because I was going out with him at the time,' Wendy explained. 'I shall just have to comfort myself with the under-manager of Woolworths, and even he seems to have changed his dinner hour.' She poked her spoon at her rice pudding and began to stir in the jam. She and Anne were having their lunch together on Monday, in Woolworths cafeteria, but without the benefit of the under-managers presence. 'Why did he have to go and change shifts? Now I shall have to haunt this place until I get him worked out again. But go on,' she said to Anne, 'Tell me all about your Saturday Night with the Stars. And I mean *all*.'

'I reserve the right not to speak,' Anne warned her solemnly.

'Spoil-sport. Get on with it. I know you went to Weymouth, the Las Vegas of the West, as it's known. By car, I presume?'

'Oh yes, and not only that, but it was yet *another* car – he seems to have one for each day and two for Sundays.'

'Well, what was it this time?'

'Quite a big car, a kind of goldy-brown colour,' Anne said vaguely.

'But what sort?'

'Oh, I don't know. I don't know anything about cars. A kind of saloon car, I suppose you'd call it.'

Wendy rolled her eyes. 'What a girl! Doesn't even know if it was a Rolls Royce Silver Cloud or a model-T Ford.'

'Neither of those,' Anne said, straight-faced. 'Something in between.'

'Give me strength! Well go on then, what did you do in Weymouth?'

'We went to the theatre,' Anne said proudly.

'Posh!' Wendy nodded. 'No back-row-of-the-flicks for Mr M. F. Conrad. Did he do it in style – best seats and everything?'

'They were good seats, I think,' Anne said. 'We could see and hear beautifully but then it is a small theatre, so I don't expect any seats are really bad. But I enjoyed it tremendously.'

'What was the play?'

'It was a comedy, a new play that's going to the West End next week. They were trying it out down here, I think. It was very funny. We both ached with laughing. It was about—'

'Never mind the play,' Wendy waved it away with a casual hand. 'I'm more interested in the details of your romance. What happened then? Tell me the worst. I can't go much greener. Not only does he look like a Martini ad, he even behaves like one. I suppose you went to dinner afterwards?'

'I'm afraid so,' Anne said. Wendy sighed.

'I thought as much,' she said resignedly. She poked her chin out and put on a nasal

129

twang. 'Okay, Doc, I can take it. Give it to me straight – right on the chin. He booked the table, didn't he?'

Anne nodded, holding back a laugh. 'Yes, he whisked me away in the golden car to a restaurant over on the other side of the harbour, where a table was booked in his name for ten-thirty, a corner table with a candle and no other lighting.'

Wendy put her head in her hands and pretended to sob. 'Go on, go on!' she groaned.

'And we had dinner, and wine, and then over the coffee and liqueurs he held my hand across the table and we talked nonsense in the nicest possible way. And then we drove home, and on the way home we stopped somewhere near Osmington, where we had a view of the sea from the car, and the moonlight was shining on the water and . . .'

She stopped, and after a moment Wendy looked up to see why, and saw Anne smiling dreamily and gazing into the distance.

'Well?' she demanded. Anne's eyes slowly refocussed.

'You don't really think I'm going to give you all the details, do you? You'll have to use your imagination for the rest.'

Wendy was eying her friend cautiously. 'I say, Anne,' she said carefully, 'you aren't really serious about this chap, are you?' Anne looked at her in surprise. 'I mean, you know, it's just a bit of fun, isn't it? We clown around and all that sort of thing, but you wouldn't be daft enough to get serious about him, would you?'

'Why do you say that?' Anne asked. Wendy laughed nervously.

'Listen, don't get upset, will you? But look, you and I both know this type of man never means anything seriously. Oh, they're great fun, taking you to the best places and so on, but he's only passing through. Has a girl in every port, and a port in every girl – you know the type.' She looked anxiously at Anne's face, trying to gauge her feelings from her expression and having no luck. 'What I'm trying to say is—'

'I think I know what you're trying to say,' Anne said quietly.

'It's just a bit of legitimate fun,' Wendy said pleadingly. 'He enjoys your company, and you enjoy his, and no harm done. When he moves on, well, that's part of his charm, isn't it? It's all charm. All those things he says – he's a salesman, isn't he?'

'A used-car salesman?' Anne suggested. Wendy looked relieved.

'That's right. And they're all a bit crooked – in the nicest possible way.'

'How can you be crooked in a nice way?' Anne said crossly. 'You think he's a con man and a crook, and probably steals cars into the bargain?'

'Now, Anne—'

'I don't know why everyone's so down on him. Just because he's a stranger in town. You're as bad as Dad. He was going on at me again yesterday, saying I couldn't trust Michael and that he'd do a moonlight flit or something, with the takings in the till. The attitude of people in this town to strangers—'

131

'Steady, steady, no need to throw bricks,' Wendy protested. Anne stopped, realising that many of the things Wendy had said had passed through her own mind.

'I'm sorry,' she said. 'But you don't know him. He's kind and thoughtful and honest and . . .'

'Yes, I know, I can see what you're trying to say,' Wendy said 'We won't talk about him any more.'

'You'd only have to meet him to know.'

'No more,' Wendy repeated firmly. 'It's none of my business anyway.' There was a silence while they both picked at their food absently. Then Wendy looked up again and said quietly, 'Only, Anne, don't get hurt, will you. He's not like Joe.'

'That's the whole point,' Anne said. And they left it at that.

Because Anne had fallen in love. It had never happened to her before, and it was quite different from any thing she had felt or imagined, different from her feelings for Joe. Michael filled her thoughts. She remembered every word he said, and the exact inflection of his voice when he said it. She relived their moments together, each kiss, each touch, each gesture. His face was always before her, so that when she looked into the mirror in the morning it was his face she saw, not her own. The sound of his voice was sweeter in her imagination than any music. She loved his name because it was his, and wrote it over and over again on her blotter just for the pleasure of writing it and reading it.

She wanted to bring him into the conversation, for the pleasure of hearing his name. She lived for the moment when she would see him again, and her life when he was not there seemed empty and flat, a mere marking time until they were together again. She saw him in the street a hundred times a day, and every time the phone rang at work or the door opened, she expected it to be him, and her heart bounded with anticipation. He might come in at any time, of course, and had she been sure he felt the same way about her as she did about him, she would have expected him first thing on Monday morning.

But of course the doubt was there to spice her excitement and happiness at being in love. Did he feel as much for her? If he did not, then she must treasure every moment she had with him against the time when he would say it was all over. If he – wonderful thought – if he was in love with her, would he tell her so, would he want to marry her, would he settle down in Market Winton, or take her to a home in some other town? She was too happy and sad and excited and anxious to worry about the details and practicalities of the possibility. All she could think of was being with him again, counting the hours until it happened, and remembering the last time they were together.

As for Wendy's gloomy warnings, and Dad's, she could not bring herself to care. Even if they were true – and she couldn't believe he was a crook, or even in the least dishonest – even if they *were* true, she still loved him, she still wanted to be with him. That he had probably

133

done this sort of thing in every town he had visited in his eventful life was the original doubt she had had, and she thrust that to the back of her mind. He *must* mean the things he said, he must! He could not say them with such conviction if it was all an act. If there had been other girls before her, still she was different, everyone fell in love some time, there was a first time for everyone, even Michael F. Conrad, Esq., bachelor-about-town.

On the whole, her happiness outweighed her worry, and she felt that she loved everyone, even Mr. Whetlore, who enquired gloomily if she was short of work, since she seemed to have time to sing songs at her desk. She smiled at everyone as she cycled past them in the morning, even said good morning to dogs and sparrows, while the postman received a rapturous greeting that made him blink and took the ache out of his fallen arches for at least five minutes afterwards.

'Someone left you a fortune, then?' he asked her, plonking the firm's mail down on her desk. 'I didn't see no birthday cards in with that lot.'

'I'm in love, postie,' she said, 'and being in love, I love everyone.'

'Cor,' he said, pushed his hat to the back of his head, and gave her a toothless smile. 'I'd 've brought you a registered letter, if I'd known, just to celebrate.'

Wendy's warning at lunchtime damped her spirits for no more than a few minutes, and she was dancing every few steps again on the way back to the office. He would come in this afternoon, certainly, she thought. He hadn't come in the morning because he wanted to give her a chance to get on with her work, but he would come in this afternoon. She looked in her mirror as she settled down at her desk again, and saw her face smiling back at her, but saw nothing else. The typewriter rippled under her fingers, and she made no mistakes in her typing. Nothing could go wrong today.

She was just about to get up and make the tea when the outer door opened and she looked up, her heart leaping. But it was not the slim dark form of Michael that came in, it was a broader shape, bronzed of skin and with sun-bleached hair. He came hesitantly across to her desk and eyed her nervously.

'Hello, Joe,' Anne greeted him gaily. She was so happy that she didn't even feel embarrassed or sad about seeing Joe again. Joe smiled back at her uncertainly, wondering perhaps what was the meaning of her smile.

'Hello, Anne.' Pause. 'You're looking well.'

'I'm feeling well. How are you, Joe? How is everything?'

'Oh, the same as usual, I suppose.'

'How are the pigs?' she asked. Joe looked hurt, and didn't answer, thinking she was making fun of him, and she elaborated the point to show him she meant it. 'Is everything all right with your job? No trouble at the farm?'

'Well,' he said slowly, still cautious, 'it's funny you should ask that, because we've had one or two of the young gilts down sick. We don't know what it is yet.'

135

'Had the vet in?'

'Yes,' he said, and unaccountably began to blush. Anne didn't know what to make of that, and went on conversationally,

'And what did he say? Did you have Mr Parker from over Magna? I hear he's very good with pigs.'

'Well no, it weren't him,' Joe said slowly. 'He was on his holidays.'

'Who did you have then?' Anne asked impatiently.

'It was the new vet from Upwood.' Anne regarded him steadily, hoping to elicit more conversation. Joe moved his eyes away from hers and continued. 'She's very young and only just started in practice. The boss said he didn't trust a young girl like that, but she seemed to know what to do all right. The gilts didn't mind her, and they're—'

'Great ones for knowing people,' Anne said, finishing one of his favourite sayings.

'They are,' he affirmed. Anne wondered at him. Was his reluctance to speak, and his blush, anything to do with the new vet being a young woman?

'Did you have much of a chat with her? What's she like?' she asked.

'She seems very nice,' Joe said, but he said it in exactly the same way as he said everyone else was nice.

'What's her name?'

'Miss Brown,' he said. His eyes met Anne's and slid away again. 'I hear you're going out with that new chap now?'

'Well, well. Doesn't news travel fast? Who told you that?'

'Oh,' he shrugged. 'It's me that people would tell, you know.'

'Yes, I suppose so.'

'Is he—' Joe hesitated, and then shook his head. 'No. I got no right to ask.'

'Is he what?' Anne urged, but Joe refused to say.

'I better go in and see Mr Whetlore, I suppose,' he said. 'With the gilts sick, I have to get back. Can you see if he'll see me?'

'Of course, Joe,' she said, and a moment later ushered him in to the Presence, as she called Mr Whetlore on his more pompous days. She didn't have much work on hand, and after she had shut the door behind Joe she sat daydreaming for a while instead of working. Michael was gone from her mind. Instead she wondered about Joe and this intriguing Lady Vet. He had seemed strangely embarrassed and reluctant to talk about her. Was it possible that he had fallen, on the rebound, as it were, for this lady who was good with pigs? And if he had, how did she, Anne, feel about it? She was still very fond of Joe, and she didn't like to think of him falling for someone else so quickly.

That sounded like very sour grapes. She wanted to think she was only concerned for his welfare, not wanting him to make a mistake, but she had to be honest and admit that she just didn't want him out with someone else. He had been her Joe for so long, it was impossible to relinquish the idea of him so soon. And yet she had fallen for

137

someone else. Perhaps Joe felt as bad about her, or worse, since he had loved more than she all along.

Of course, on the other hand, it might just be that he was embarrassed to talk about the lady vet in case Anne thought exactly what she had thought, that there was something in it.

'Well, either way,' Anne told herself severely, 'it's none of your damn business. You've made sure of that now. Joe wouldn't take you back now you've taken up with a stranger so soon after finishing with him.' And then she wondered why she should even think about going back with Joe.

Joe wasn't in with Mr Whetlore for long. He stopped by Anne's desk on his way out.

'Well, is everything all right? I've had a look at the papers, and it seems quite promising,' Anne said.

'Yes, I think it will be all right,' Joe said.

'You don't seem very excited. Is something wrong?'

'Oh, no, no.'

'Price too high?'

'Well, it's high, but I'll manage. No, it isn't that.'

'Then what is it?'

'Nothing, there's nothing wrong,' Joe said, but he seemed depressed. 'I—'

'What?'

'Nothing.' He turned to go. 'Goodbye, Anne.' It sounded terribly final.

'Will you have a cup of tea before you go?' Anne asked. She didn't want him to go away so sad.

'No thanks, I must go. I want to catch the library before it closes. It closes early on a Monday.'

'What are you going there for?' Anne asked in frank curiosity.

'See if I can get a book,' he said.

'I didn't know you were a reader,' Anne said in surprise. While they had been going out together, he had never read more than the occasional paper. 'What book are you looking for?'

'It's called *Capital*. It's by Karl Marx.'

Anne stared and blinked. 'Karl Marx? What on earth do you want to read Karl Marx for?'

Joe looked offended. 'I'm not an ignoramus, you know. I can read.'

'Yes, but—'

'I'm interested in Socialism. Well, all politics really, but Socialism and Economics mostly.'

'Good gracious,' was all Anne could say.

'Irene recommended me to read up about the beginnings of it and she told me that book. We had quite a long talk about it. She's interested in it too.'

'Irene, I presume, is the vet,' Anne said faintly.

'Miss Brown,' Joe confitmed, his boldness leaking away and leaving him shy again. 'I have to go now,' he said, and made a bolt for the door.

'Goodbye,' Anne said, and she felt it was as final as his goodbye had been a moment ago. It seemed she had not known him very well after all. She had never had any idea he was interested in anything other than pigs. This Miss Brown had found out more about him in one visit than she had in four years.

Unless, of course, the interest in socialism dated from the discovery of Miss Irene Brown's interest in it. But either way, it looked as though Joe was gone for good. She told herself she ought to be pleased that he had found someone else without too much heartache, but it was an effort.

By the time she was ready to go home, a lot of her cheerfulness had evaporated, and she had a splitting headache. Michael had not come in during the afternoon nor phoned her, and the noise of the typewriter seemed to have hammered into her head like horseshoe-nails. She covered up her typewriter wearily and stood up, and had to grab her desk to stop herself falling, for she was dizzy. She hung onto it for a moment as the blackness receded in that horribly slow way it had, and then shook her head and immediately wished she hadn't. Dear me, you are an up and downer, she told herself wryly. This morning on top of the world, this afternoon in the depths.

She cycled slowly at first, afraid she might feel dizzy again, but she seemed to be all right, and put it down to standing up too quickly. Her head still ached, though, and she decided to stop off in the village on her way home for some aspirin. The chemist was still open, and she went in there for them. It was a lovely shop, a big brown dignified shop, with *Moore Bros.* in curly gold writing along the shopfront, and those huge coloured-glass jars in the windows among dusty displays of perfumes and talcum powder. It was still run by a Mr Moore, a nephew of the one who had painted *Est. 1898* over the door. He was now nearly sixty and had lived in the village since he was ten, so he knew everyone, and all their business, and could give them pretty sound advice on their various ailments, with which he was also well acquainted.

Anne went into the cool, scented gloom of the shop and, since he was busy serving old Mrs Benson, or rather listening to her talk, she leaned on the counter with her eyes half closed, gazing idly at the various displays around her. Mr Moore had a nice way of combining the old and the new in medicine. The front counter was laid out with all the modern proprietory drugs in their bright tempting packets, all the well-known names, and the bottles with the white labels marked BP which used to puzzle her as a child, for she couldn't think what they had to do with Scouts.

But behind the counter were the other things that many of the villagers still relied on – tall jars of coltsfoot rock and liquorice; small, glass-stoppered jars of herbs, pennyroyal and rosemary and peppermint and marsh-mallow; and the little, square, gold-lettered drawers with those mysterious and exotic-sounding names, alum, and borax, and Flowers of Sulphur. Dreaming there in the cool of his shop, Anne could imagine herself coming in dressed in flowers like Ophelia and buying a pinch of pennyroyal and a shilling's worth of borax in little twists of paper, as she had bought sherbert and hundreds-and-thousands as a child . . .

'And what can I do for you, Anne?' Mr Moore's

141

deep voice broke across her dream and startled her back to reality.

'Oh! Sorry, I was dreaming, I was miles away. Well, about a hundred yards away, to be exact, at Mrs Fathom's sweetie shop, when I was a kid.'

'Ah yes, dear old Ma Fathom. Passed on ten years since, but still missed,' Mr Moore acquiesced with the ease of long practice to her random thought.

'I only came in for some aspirin. I had a splitting headache, but it's eased just standing here – it's so cool and peaceful.'

'Well, if it's just a headache you've got, have a sniff of this. He reached behind him for a small jar, which he unstoppered and held out to her. 'Close your eyes and have a good long smell of this. Gently.'

She held the jar to her nose and breathed in, a half-familiar, herbal smell. 'What is it?' she asked.

'Never mind, have another sniff.' She did so. 'It's rosemary,' he told her. She opened her eyes.

'So it is.'

'The best thing for headaches. My Aunt Sybil used to have a great bush of it in her garden, and whenever she got a headache she'd go out and run her hands over the bush and then have a good sniff. Cleared it away like one-o'clock.'

'Is that the Aunt that ran this shop with your uncle?'

'That's right, marvellous woman. Knew everything there is to know about herbs. Pity really she didn't write it down, pass it on. Nowadays

142

everyone writes books. It would have sold a million. Made wine out of anything that came to hand, too. How's the headache?'

Anne thought. 'It's gone,' she marvelled.

'There you are. I've done myself out of a sale. Never mind, I won't be here much longer.'

'You aren't thinking of going are you?' Anne cried, aghast. 'Winton Parva without a Mr Moore to cure its ailments—'

'Chemist shop doesn't pay any more. Ask anyone. Losing money hand over fist. I don't mind. I've not got much longer to go, and I've my bit put aside; I shall retire and grow vegetables and go fishing. Love fishing – no time to do it. Chemist has to work all hours, when he's needed. But the government don't pay enough. Costs money to fill prescriptions. Only way to keep going is diversify, sell all that fancy stuff, like the big chain shops in the towns. I'm too old for that lark. No, I'll just keep going a year longer, then I'll pull out. They can turn this into a supermarket when I'm gone.'

'Oh no,' Anne said, 'it would be a crying shame. Such a lovely shop! I was thinking that as I came in. All the lovely polished wood and the gold lettering.'

'Original,' Mr Moore said proudly. 'But it doesn't pay. Got to be sharp nowadays to make business pay. Talking of which, what about that Mr Conrad?'

'What about him?' Anne said, astonished. Not astonished that he knew, but that he had brought it up so abruptly, in mid-flow as it were.

'He's a sharp one, so I've heard. City boy

– slick. I should watch him, if I were you. You can't be too careful, pretty young girl like you.'

Anne flushed red, torn between anger at his interference and gratitude for his care. 'He's all right,' she said briefly. No use piling on the praise where it wouldn't be appreciated, or believed. 'And I am careful.'

'Hmm.' He nodded, closing the subject with more delicacy than she might have expected. 'You're looking a bit flushed. I think you might have one of these summer colds coming on. Stay in bed tomorrow if you don't feel well. Too many people go to work and spread the germs, not to say delay their own recovery.'

'I'll remember what you say,' Anne said. 'And perhaps I'll take some aspirin after all, in case the headache comes back.'

'Right you are. So I didn't lose a sale after all. Keep you chatting long enough and you'll buy up the shop, eh?' She smiled at his little joke, aware of her red face and the returning headache, and wondering what to attribute them to – embarrassment, or virus.

Ten

Anne knew, as soon as she woke up the next morning, that she had a cold. Mr Moore's diagnosis had been accurate, as usual. She didn't feel too bad, but bearing in mind what he had said, she stayed in bed, and when Dad came in to see her she told him that she would not be going in to work.

'I've got a cold, and I think I might shake it off if I stay home today.'

'Sensible girl,' her father approved. 'No use going in to work today and being off all week for it. I'll phone them up for you and tell them you won't be in.'

'Thanks, Dad. It's all right, there isn't much on at the moment.'

'Of course it's all right,' he said soothingly. 'Now, is there anything you want?'

'Not just now, Dad. I think I'll go back to sleep for a while.'

'That's right, dear. I won't disturb you.'

He crept out on tiptoes, and Anne smiled lovingly at his careful back. He loved to fuss over her, but rarely had the chance. She closed · her eyes and snuggled down again, and was soon asleep.

She woke mid-morning to find herself very uncomfortable. She was too hot, and sweating and turning restlessly had made a mess of her bed. The sheets were wrinkled and damp, her head ached, her nose was stuffy, and she was parched with thirst. She was relieved now that she hadn't gone in to work, but she felt too miserable to feel very glad about it. She dozed again, lightly, and then Dad came in, and she felt a great relief at seeing him, for she was feeling lonely, as people ill in bed do.

'How are you feeling, love?' he asked her in the hushed tone of a sick-visitor.

'Thirsty,' she said, picking one symptom from the many.

'Shall I make you a cup of tea?' he asked, brightening. 'Or would you rather a cold drink?'

'A couple of aspirin and a cup of tea,' she said. 'Thanks Dad.'

His thoughtfulness made her feel, in her weakened state, tearful, for when he returned with the tea he brought it not in the usual 'shaving mug' but in the pretty white china mug with the pink briar-rose hand-painted on it, a present from a school friend some while ago. And having put down the mug on her bedside table, he tugged the wrinkles out of her sheets, straightened the covers, and plumped up her pillows, leaving her at once more comfortable and less fretful.

'Now, here's your aspirin, and there's your tea. How are you feeling? How's the cold?'

'Oh, ripening nicely, Anne said, attempting a smile. 'You are good to me, Dad, really you are.'

He looked embarrassed. 'I'm your father, I'm supposed to be good to you,' he said. 'Now, is there anything else you want? I'm just going to pop out on my bike for a while. I'll only be about half an hour, and then I'll make you some lunch.'

'I don't think I feel like eating,' she said mildly, though the thought of food was very off-putting.

'Well, we'll see,' said her father, exactly as he had replied to her more outrageous childhood demands. 'So there's nothing you want just now?'

'No, I'm fine now, thanks.'

When he had gone, she lay back and listened to the unusual silence of late morning on a working day. She only ever heard it when she was ill, or occasionally on holiday, for on all other working days she was in the office with the clatter of the typewriter and the shrilling of the phones. A sparrow outside the window chirped like a squeaky wheel, and far away a dog barked with a monotonous, heat-dazed sound. The sunlight fell still and heavy outside her window, showing up the layer of dust on it, and everything else was quiet and empty, as though the world had been deserted for some other place more full of action.

Anne felt bored, but was too weighed-down with the lassitude of her cold to want to do anything. It was a dreary kind of feeling, and lonely too. She felt very sorry for herself, and though she knew this was only a symptom like the others, it still made her eyes fill with tears. But the tears hung there for a moment and then faded away. She was too dull even to cry, and besides, her nose was too stuffy for

147

crying to be pleasurable. She dozed again, waking every few minutes to hear the same sparrow cheeping and the small village noises very far away and muted.

When Dad came home, she heard him from the moment he opened the gate, right through the house until he came into her room, looking very pleased with himself.

'Hullo, love. I've brought you some things,' he said.

'Is that what you went out for?' she asked, pushing herself up on one elbow and feeling very dopey.

'Well, half and half,' he admitted, smiling. 'I got you some oranges – they're good for colds. Vitamin C, you can't get too much of it.' He took the six oranges out of the bag, and their pungent, maddening smell got through even her nose blockade.

'Thanks, Dad,' she said. He dug further in the bag. 'What else?'

'Some Vick to rub on your chest – that'll help you breathe too,' he said, thoroughly enjoying himself, 'and some lemon barley water, you ought to drink plenty when you've a cold. You know you tend to run to throats, and drinking a lot's important to keep your glands clear.' The bag was deflating now, but he still had something more, for his expression was that of a conjurer who saves the rabbit until last.

'And then,' he said triumphantly, 'I went to the library and got you some books to read. I know how you're always at the books, and I knew you'd be lost without them.'

'You are kind,' Anne said, feeling tearful again.

'I didn't know what you'd like, but that nice girl Jennie was on duty, and she knows what you usually take out. She said you could have as many as you liked, and not to worry about tickets. She's a nice girl. Oh, and I saw your young man there too.'

Michael's face came before her eyes like a flash of light as he said that, but before she could speak he went on,

'Or perhaps I should say your ex-young-man. Joe.'

Oh. Of course, it would be Joe. Her heart sank down again into it's usual place. 'What was he doing there?' she asked with an effort.

'Standing in front of a bookshelf taking down all sorts of massive great books that didn't look as if they'd been read since the year dot. I said hello to him, and then I kidded him a bit. Asked him if he'd broken a table leg or something.' Dad grinned at his own humour. 'Don't think he got it, though. He just looked at me as if someone had hit him on the head with one of 'em.'

'I think he's taken to reading in the long summer evenings,' Anne said. 'I'm grateful for the books, anyway, Dad – I was feeling bored, but too dopey to do anything. You know how it is.'

'I know,' her father said sympathetically. 'Well, you may get a visitor to cheer you up.' Again, momentarily, her thoughts flew to Michael. 'I told Joe you were poorly, and he said he'd try to pop in and have a chat. Anyway, love, I must go across for the 12.30 or I'll be out of a job.'

He left her thoughtful as his familiar,

149

unmistakable step-and-thud receded through the house. Dear old Dad, hoping still that she and Joe would get back together again, hoping that visiting her on her bed of suffering would melt his heart and make her realise how she had missed him. How little he dreamt that that was now impossible, how little he realised where her heart was and what it fed on. She wanted Michael to come and visit her, but she had no way to get in touch with him. She could hardly ask Dad to phone him at his hotel – and she wouldn't want him to anyway.

But he would probably call in at the office some time during the day, and then he'd know she was ill. Surely he would call around? He'd come to enquire how she was and if he could see her. Dad wasn't especially welcoming, but he would't let that put him off. If he were ill she'd force her way in against armed guards if necessary. He would come. Perhaps this evening.

The day dragged on, and she felt worse. It was one of those colds that develops quickly; she hoped it would clear up as quickly too. Dad popped in and out between trains fetching her drinks and straightening her bed. She read a little, but it made her head ache. She stared at the dusty window and grew irritated by it and longed to clean it. She dozed and woke stupefied.

At last the sounds of the day quickened and cooled into evening. The sky paled from its brassy blue and the trees moved around and rustled like people gossiping on their way home from work. With the cooling of the air Anne felt

150

better, though more remote. She thought it must be getting on for tea time, when Dad poked his head round the door.

'Visitor for you,' he announced smugly. 'Do you want to tidy yourself up a bit first?'

'Oh yes, please,' she said, struggling up. 'Who is it?'

'Surprise,' Dad said. Could it be Michael? But then Dad wouldn't be so pleased. Yet if it was Joe, why did he say 'surprise' when he had already told her he might call? Her mind wavered between hope and doubt as she dragged a comb through her hair and rubbed her face with the damp flannel Dad brought her. He bolstered up her pillows again and brought her a cardigan to slip on, both against the evening cool and for the sake of decency.

'I'll make you some tea, too,' he said. 'You've had nothing all day. Could you eat a boiled egg?'

'Yes, all right. Just one. And a piece of bread and butter,' Anne agreed.

'Nice thin bread and butter,' Dad said, smiling. 'For the invalid. Ready for your visitor now?'

Her heart plunged upwards on a crest of hope, and tumbled down again in disappointment as Joe came in, pink and scrubbed after work, his hair still spiky with the wet comb he had used to try to discipline it, and in his hand a bunch of bluebells.

'The last from the wood up Haldane's,' he said by way of greeting, holding out the flowers to her. 'They don't last long, poor things, but they smell nice.'

151

'I can't smell anything with this wretched cold, but it was kind of you to bring them,' Anne said ruefully. 'Please sit down. You don't need to act like a visitor here.'

'I'd better put these in some water first,' he said. 'They'll die else.' He went out and came back again a moment later, presumably having asked Dad for a vase. He put the flowers down on her bedside table, picked up one of the books that was lying there and read the title, smiled absently and put it down again, and then remembered his manners.

'Um, how are you? Are you feeling bad?'

'Pretty awful, but it's only a cold. Dreary while it lasts, but no mortal danger.'

'That's good,' Joe said without smiling. He sat down at her bedside and stared at the pillow behind her head. 'Your Dad told me you were ill, so I thought I'd come and see you,' he said with an effort.

'Yes, Dad told me,' she said.

'You seemed all right yesterday,' he said. 'Chirpy, I thought.' He sounded almost resentful, she thought, as if she had no right to be chirpy when she ought to be ill.

'I think that was probably feverishness,' she said. He nodded.

'I was glad to see you chirpy,' he went on as if she hadn't spoken. 'I worried about you.'

'Did you, Joe?'

'Yes, I did. I know it isn't my business any more, but well, when you love someone, you can't help feeling it is even if it isn't, if you know what I mean.'

'Yes, I know what you mean,' Anne said, thinking of Michael. 'But I rather thought you had other fish to fry now?'

'How's that?' Joe seemed puzzled, and she didn't want to bring the vet into the conversation; it would sound bitchy.

'Forget it,' she said. 'Anyway, you don't need to worry about me, Joe. I'm all right. Other than this cold.'

'Are you?' he asked significantly. 'Because, you see, I was wondering about that bloke you've been going out with. I know it's none of my business—'

'People always say that when they're about to make it so,' Anne complained. Joe ignored the interruption.

'But I just felt I ought to warn you about him.'

'Oh, not again! These warnings are getting to be very monotonous,' Anne said irritably.

'Again? I never—'

'You aren't the first,' Anne said grimly. 'How this town loves a stranger! He's done nothing worse than arrive here from another place, but already he's been put down as the worst villain outside of Wormwood Scrubs. I wouldn't be surprised if the police haven't got a couple of plain-clothes men trailing him all day, waiting for him to commit a crime.'

'I don't know about that,' Joe said, injured. 'I wouldn't say he was a criminal. I don't know anything about him.'

'Then why judge him?' Anne snapped.

'You don't think I'd repeat gossip, do you?' Joe said, affronted. Anne didn't quite grasp the import of that, but she was too cross to wonder about it.

'You may have had the best of motives, which I don't doubt,' she said, 'but until the day I come to you to warn you about lady vets also new to the district, and doubtless very sinister silences sticking out from every sentence she utters, don't come to me with warnings about city slickers taking me for a ride. I've been for a ride with him in several of his cars, and I intend to go on several more.'

Joe was on his dignity now. He stood up, towering above her like a bronze and gold statue of a Greek god, beautiful and powerful and, at the moment, utterly infuriating.

'I'm sorry I upset you,' he said slowly. 'I'd better go.'

She didn't reply, and after a moments hesitation he turned and left her. She flung herself over onto her side in petulant anger, and came up against his bunch of wilting bluebells, beautiful still even though they were dying. She turned away onto her other side and wept a few bitter tears. In a while Dad put his head round the door and said,

'Oh, is Joe gone? I was just looking into ask if he wanted to have his tea with you.'

'He had to go,' Anne said dully. 'He was busy.'

'Oh, that's a shame. Never mind, love. I'll put a nice tea on a tray for you. Won't be a sec.'

And when he came in again, it was with a tray laid with a tray cloth that hadn't been out of the linen cupboard since Mother died. And there was a brown boiled egg in her cockerel egg-cup, and thin bread and butter, and strawberry jam, and a cup of tea, all arranged nicely on the tray, and on the best china. The final touch was that one of the slices of bread had been cut, meticulously, into 'soldiers' for dipping into her egg. Anne managed to smile her gratitude at him, but as soon as he had departed, the tears rolled freely down her face. There was a quality to his kindness that nearly broke her heart.

Anne woke the next morning with a very nasty sore throat, and Dad was worried enough about her to telephone for Dr Ross. He came about mid-morning when Anne was listening in a bored way to the radio and flicking over the pages of a detective novel.

'Living the life of Riley, aren't you?' he said cheerfully. 'What wouldn't I give for a day or two in bed?'

'You can have it,' she croaked, 'whatever it is.'

'Laryngitis,' he said briskly. 'Soon cure that. I'll give your Dad a prescription for some penicillin. The old Wonder Drug, you know. That'll have you on your feet right as ninepence in no time at all.'

'How long is no time at all?' Anne enquired, having known him nearly all her life.

'You'll be back to work on Monday. I should take the rest of the week off. I know that throat of yours. Stay in bed for a couple of days, and then just rest. I'll give the prescription to your Dad, and he can run it down to Moore's. I'd take it myself, but I'm going the other way. Cheerio, then, Anne – keep your pecker up.'

Dad obligingly phoned the news through to Anne's bosses, and went down to Moore's on his bike with the prescription. Anne was not too worried by the sore throat or the accompanying symptoms, nor even by missing a week at work, but she was afraid she was going to be driven mad with boredom. She was very glad therefore to get a visitor at lunch time.

'I've given up my entire lunch break to come and soothe your bed of pain,' Wendy said, gusting into the bedroom on a cloud of perfume and sitting on the side of the bed. 'Isn't that kind of me?'

'Very kind,' Anne agreed as best she could.

'My God that sounds terrible! What is it you've got? I hope it's not catching,' Wendy said, and without obliging Anne to reply, went on, 'I telephoned you at work today, or rather tried to, but of course you weren't there. Old Wetdrawers said that your Dad had just that moment phoned to say you were on your deathbed and not likely to be back at work until the millennium, so I had this idea of incredible nobility and generosity.' She struck her chest proudly. 'I get these attacks from time to time. It's in my nature.'

'Who drove you down here?'

'Who did what?' Wendy said, sounding incredulous and hurt. Anne smiled.

'You wouldn't have come if you'd had to use the bus,' she croaked.

'There's gratitude for you! Heap someone up with kindness, and they spit in your eye! Well, it was Roberto actually,' she said modestly. Anne made who's Roberto noises, and she went on, 'He's the new waiter in the Italian restaurant. His name's Robert actually – he isn't Italian, of course, just looks it. He's from Blandford. He worked in a Wimpey bar there, and this is a step up for him, so he's practising the accent in case he can get a job in an Italian restaurant in London. That's his ambition. So I call him Roberto, because he says it helps him if he *thinks* Italian, and you can't think Italian if someone's tugging your elbow and calling you Bob all the time.'

She paused for breath. 'And he calls me Lucia – you know, like in the song *Santa Loochee-a* – because he says there's absolutely nothing you can do with Wendy in Italian. You can't even say it with an Italian accent.'

'Where's Roberto now? Why didn't you bring him in?'

'He's gone back to town. He'll come and collect me later,' Wendy said. 'You'll never guess who I saw last night.'

'Whom.'

'Whom I saw, last night, in Roberto's restaurant.'

'Were you eating there? How expensive of you.'

'Oh, no, I wasn't eating there. I was waiting for Roberto to come off duty, and I peeped out through the service hatch and right over in the corner at a table with a candle I saw . . .'

Anne's memory conjured up a vivid picture of that night in Weymouth, the little table with the candle and Michael reaching across to take her hand.

'. . . your Mr M. F. Conrad, in person, noshing in style on the best the menu can offer. Though the most expensive thing on the menu's only £2.50, which can't compare with some of the places he must have been. I'll bet when he took you to Weymouth it cost more than that. Still, this isn't Weymouth, and it's a lot better than taking her to the Forum Caff for egg and chips, like old Joe did with you.'

'Who?'

'Who who?'

'Who was M. F. Conrad buying dinner for in the Italian restaurant?' Anne asked carefully. Wendy shrugged indifferently.

'Oh I don't know. Some girl or other. She looked Italian, though judging by my experience with Roberto, that probably means she comes from Winterbourne Zelstone and talks like something off the Archers.'

Anne felt dizzy, though Wendy didn't at first notice and went on prattling gaily about nothing in particular. Anne found her heart hammering in a most peculiar way. She tried to tell herself that it was nothing, that Wendy was mistaken, but she knew that wasn't true. Wendy couldn't possibly mistake Michael, she had stared at him too often for that. It must be true: and all the warnings she had been given had been given in vain. He was the kind of man who always had several girls on a string, and if one failed him, another took her place. She had been warned about him almost from the beginning, but she had still foolishly, foolhardily, gone ahead and fallen in love with him. Never love

158

a stranger, they had all said in their various ways, even poor Joe, who had no reason to feel kindly about her.

He had presumably discovered that she was ill, and, far from hurrying to see her, as Wendy had, and dear, kind Joe, had immediately set about fixing himself up with someone else to take her place. Anne felt rather sick at the thought of her own feelings for him, and the fool she might have made of herself, and as she closed her eyes against the rush of nausea, Wendy at last noticed there was something wrong.

'Here, you don't look quite the thing,' she said anxiously. 'You've gone all pale – are you all right, Anne? Shall I call your Dad?' She took Anne's hand and patted it anxiously, and Anne closed her fingers round the comforting grasp and shook her head.

'No, it's nothing. I'm all right. I'll be all right in a minute. It's just—' She opened her eyes and looked at Wendy who, for all her pretended insensitivity must have read something of the trouble in Anne's expression.

'Listen, you're not upset about you-know-who, are you? Listen, Anne, you mustn't take anything like that to heart. You know what those kind of fellers are. They mean every word of what they say when they're saying it. It's just that they say it ten times a week to ten different girls. You didn't take it seriously, now, did you? Tell your old Aunty Wendy you don't mind it? He can't help it, poor soul, it's just the way he is. I'm the same myself, never could settle for one flower when there's so many to flit round.'

She sounded really anxious, and Anne tried to smile and shook her head again.

'No, no, it's nothing like that,' she said, but even as she said it the tears began to seep out from her eyes, and they both knew she was lying.

Eleven

After that, she could hardly expect a visit from Michael, and she told herself that she did not expect it. Why then, when her father announced a visitor for her on Friday, did her heart leap so treacherously?

'I was passing, so I thought I'd drop in and see you,' said the doctor. 'You don't look as well as I expected. Not up yet?'

'Oh, I'm all right,' she said listlessly. 'I'm just being lazy I suppose.'

'Well you certainly sound better as far as the voice goes. I expect it's the penicillin making you droopy. Let's see the throat. Hmm. Yes, well that seems to have cleared itself up, doesn't it? Keep taking the tablets until they're all gone anyway, just to make sure.'

'Yes, I will,' Anne said.

'You sound in the dumps,' Dr Ross said sternly. 'I'm all for taking it easy when the patient benefits from it, but in your case I'd say you were feeling a wee bit too sorry for yourself. I think you should get up, get dressed and go for a nice walk. It's a lovely day.'

'Nowhere to go,' Anne said childishly. There's nothing worse than being talked to briskly when you're feeling sunk in the depths of gloom.

'You can go and have a look at a little cottage I've seen for sale across at Little Hotham. That's

161

only half a mile by the fields. I thought it would just do nicely for you and your Dad.'

'Why for us?' Anne asked, pricking up her ears with interest.

'I had it from Moore. Apparently your father was talking to him when he took the prescription in, about the business of British Rail turfing you out. He reckoned – your Dad, that is – that if he could find an alternative place to that bungalow that wasn't too expensive, he might be able to persuade them to buy it for him instead.'

'That sounds like a possible plan,' Anne said without too much hope. 'Where is this place?'

'It more or less faces the railway line, just beyond the triple bridge, you know where I mean, where that big house with the tall chimney is. You can't see the cottage until you're right up to it because of the hedges round the big house, but from the cottage you can see the railway line perfectly.'

'It sounds ideal,' Anne said with a laugh.

'It is a nice little place,' the doctor said. 'It's been modernised – one of my new patients bought it and did it up, but he didn't like the idea of an outside toilet, even though it is a proper mains-drain flushing job. So he moved. It's on the market now, and I dare say it wouldn't be too expensive. The only thing I wonder is if you'd find it a bit small for the two of you. My patient was a widower and not likely to remarry. Lived there with his dog and was snug as a bug in a rug, but you and your Dad might find it a thought *too* snug. I don't know.'

'Have you told Dad about it?'

'I told him. He said he'd go and have a look, but he sounded a bit gloomy about it. Just like you did *before* I told you. See how much more cheerful you are now you're thinking of someone else and not yourself.'

'You're always right,' Anne said. 'Don't you get sick of it?'

'How could I? It's my job to be right. Anyway. I must get on now – I've been gassing to you long enough. Get out and get some fresh air, and don't be moping around in your room. Cheerio for now.'

In the end, Anne and her father both went to see the cottage after lunch. Dad on his bike with Anne on the crossbar. 'We can walk back,' he said, 'if you feel you need the exercise.'

It was a dear little cottage, a real Dorset cottage, cob-ended and newly thatched, with the thatch decorations of the local man. Each thatcher decorated his roofs in his own style so that everyone knew who had done them and the Winton man was one of the old Dorset Catholic families, and always decorated the centre of the ridge with a stylised plaited cross. The cottage had been whitewashed, and the window frames painted smart black, bold against the white stone. The garden was rather overgrown, as could be expected, and was sweet with honeysuckle that rioted everywhere and attracted the bees for miles around. They couldn't get into the cottage, of course, but they walked through to the back garden, and found it in better order, having been dug for vegetables before the owner left it. The toilet was discreetly tucked away down a side path and again decorated with honeysuckle, and there was a damson tree in the middle of the small lawn.

'It's beautiful,' Anne said enthusiastically. 'Really, I can't imagine why anyone would want to leave it, outside loo or no outside loo.'

'Mm,' Dad said non-committally, but taking a glance at him, Anne saw that he loved it, that it was the kind of place he would have chosen if he had limitless choice. It was built for him, absolutely, it would fit round him like his own body now fitted round his heart. The only thing was, as the doctor had said, that it was very small. It was so small it was like a dolls' house, and standing in the garden in the front one could touch the bottom of the upstairs window.

'I wonder if we can get permission to view it,' she mused. She had been inside a similar cottage before, and thought that it would probably have one room downstairs and two tiny ones upstairs. The kitchen was housed in a single-storey extension at the back, and the bath would be a tin one, stood on the kitchen floor when needed and filled with kettles. As doctor said, really a bit too small for her and Dad.

'Too small,' Dad said as if echoing her thoughts, but she heard the sigh in his voice as he said it.

'No harm in going to have a look at it, anyway,' Anne said.

'No, no harm.'

'After all, you never know,' Anne said. She said it only vaguely to cheer him up without meaning anything, but his expression brightened at once and he said more cheerfully,

164

'No, you never know. After all . . .'

After all, he meant, you might still marry Joe. After all, Anne added for herself he did come and visit you on your sickbed, which was more than that fancy chap from London did, for all his money and big cars. She knew the lines off by heart, having said them all to herself in preparation. Not that Dad would say them aloud unless she provoked him, but she knew he was thinking them, and that was almost as bad.

On Friday night Anne was watching the television and half-heartedly repairing a pair of tights when there was a knock on the door. She was startled for a moment, and then, dredging up from the depths of her subconscious memory the sound of a car, she thought it was probably Joe come to visit her again. She jumped up, eager for company, and not at all sorry to see Joe again, even after their last meeting. After all, he had been proved right, hadn't he? And he'd only meant it for the best at the time.

She opened the front door (Dad was across at the station) and at once her heart gave such a lurch that she thought she would literally faint. She clutched the door-knob until her fingers went white, and stared at him without being able to speak for a moment.

'Hello, can I come in?' Michael said, having waited for her to speak first. Anne still could not speak. He cocked his head on one side and said, 'Am I intruding? Say at once if you'd rather I didn't interrupt.' Was he suggesting she had someone else in there? she thought, outraged. She shook her head.

'I'm alone,' she said. He smiled pleasantly and nudged her gently out of the way, since she didn't look as though she was going to move. She turned her head to follow him, and the light struck her face.

'I say, you don't look very bright,' he said with concern. 'Are you ill?'

That was pretty cool, coming from him, she thought. But then coolness was to be expected from the expert.

'I've had laryngitis,' she said coldly. He drew his hands out from behind him and presented her with a beautiful bunch of flowers.

'In that case, my present is doubly appropriate. I do hope you're better.'

'Yes, thank you,' she said. She took the flowers with an automatic gesture. They were roses, pink roses, three shades of pink, tied up in a florist's wrapper. Hothouse roses, of course, this early in the year – or imported. Expensive anyway. 'I should have thought you'd know I was ill,' she said.

He walked ahead of her into the sitting room, and she followed him, wondering why she didn't just tell him to go. But of course her turncoat heart knew the answer to that. At the sight and sound of him, her heart had resumed its stupid, blind, pigheaded love of him, despite anything her mind could say.

'How could I know?' he said easily. 'I've been away. Or didn't you notice?' he regarded her with his bright, level gaze. 'Ah, is that the reason

166

for the Big Frost? You didn't know I'd gone away, and you thought I was neglecting you on your sickbed?'

'How could I know you were away?' she echoed him. 'You didn't tell me.' She half wanted him to explain, was half afraid that he would tell a lie she'd see through.

'I was going to send you a note,' he said, settling himself with charming ease on the sofa and patting the seat beside him. She seated herself, as a compromise, on the nearest armchair to him. 'To tell you I'd be away. But then I thought, why waste words? She'll know I'm away when she doesn't see me. And if she doesn't notice that she hasn't seen me for a while, it will prove she doesn't care a jot for me and then I can throw myself off the nearest bridge.'

Anne turned her face away to hide her feelings. It was too bad of him to sound as if he cared whether or not *she* cared. He saw the gesture, but misread it.

'But I wasn't to know that while I was away, my beloved would be struck down with – whatever was it?'

'Laryngitis,' she said, and it sounded foolish.

'Very nasty,' he said solemnly. 'Laryngitis, anyway, and be cut to the quick that I had left her to die alone. My very humblest apologies,' he finished, contriving to bow from the waist while remaining seated. 'Had I known I'd have been making use of the opportunity to bring you hothouse grapes and nectarines and wild strawberries and bottles of rare oriental cordial. I always wanted to buy you things.'

Instead, thought Anne, you made use of the opportunity to fix yourself up with someone germ-free.

'Where did you go, then?' she asked, trying not to sound interested.

'Up to Birmingham,' he said easily. 'Mecca of the motor car. The home of the internal combustion engine. I had various people I had to let know about my new enterprise here. I hope to be agent for one or two firms; that pays the rent quite nicely while other bits and pieces provide the profit.'

'And when did you go?'

'This is beginning to sound like the Grand Inquisition—' When did you last see your father?' he clowned. 'On Monday night, star of my East, on Monday night.'

Anne turned her face towards him then, and all her bitterness must have been in her eyes as she said, quietly but firmly, 'Yet you were in a restaurant here in Winton on Tuesday night with a dark-haired lady.'

There was quite a long silence, while Michael stared at her. His expression was one of surprise, but that might be surprise that she knew. And was he, in that long silence, working out what to say? At last he said, quietly,

'Who tells you so.'

'You were seen,' she said flatly. There was another pause while he stared at her again, and a strange expression flickered across his face. She didn't quite know what it was. Could it be disappointment in her? Then he got up and walked across to the window and stood there

168

with his back to her. She saw that his hands were clenched into fists. Guilt? Or anger?

'Well,' she said at last, 'aren't you going to try and justify yourself?'

'Do you consider being in a restaurant with a dark-haired lady something that needs justification? Is it a crime?' he asked. Anne looked at his back and was glad that he could not see her face.

'No, not at all. I have no right to say who you should dine with. But what I think needs justifying is that you should lie about it to me. If you have to lie, then it means it must be something you're ashamed of.'

'Not necessarily,' he said, turning round. His face was dark with some emotion she did not understand, and his eyes were bright and dangerous. 'I can think of many reasons why I might not tell you I dined with a dark-haired lady. A secret is not, of itself, a guilty thing.'

'Then why did you keep it secret?'

'Keep what secret?' he asked.

'Dining with the dark-haired lady,' she said angrily. 'Don't prevaricate.'

'My dear Miss Symons, wherever I was on Tuesday night, it was not in Winton dining at a restaurant with a dark-haired lady.'

'You deny it?'

'I certainly don't deny it. It isn't a matter for denial,' he said with a spark of anger. 'I simply tell you that I was not there.'

'Why should I believe that?' she asked bitterly. 'I was told you were there by someone who saw you.'

'What you believe is your own affair,' he said calmly. 'As I see it you have two alternatives. You can believe this – friend, for want of a better word – who tells you she saw me. Or you can believe me, when I tell you I wasn't there. And before you ask me for proof,' he said, anticipating her opened mouth, 'let me tell you that I have no intention of attempting to prove anything. Your belief or disbelief must come from yourself. I wouldn't stoop to try to prove it.'

'I wasn't going to ask for proof,' Anne said more mildly. 'I was just going to ask you how you know the person who told me was a she.'

'Intuition, my dear Watson,' he said grinning infectiously, just as if they weren't having a bitter quarrel. 'Only a she would bring tales like that to you.'

'Oh,' Anne said. She paused to try and sort out her thoughts, and could not, and looked up at Michael for his help. Make it easy for me, her eyes pleaded, make up my mind for me.

'You're on your own, kid,' he said, but he said it gently, looking down at her almost as if he felt sorry for her. 'Belief comes from inside. You've only got to show me the door if you want me to go.'

Wendy had seemed to be telling the truth. Why would she lie? How could she be mistaken? On the other hand, Michael seemed to be telling the truth too. The very fact that he would not argue with her had a ring of truth about it. *Belief comes from inside.* Which of them did she believe? The stranger she knew so little about? Or the friend she had known for so long? Which did she care more about – the casual friend she had coffee with, or the man she had fallen in love with, whom, even now, she ached to kiss.

And while she wondered, her eyes remained fixed on his face, and after a moment he took a step towards her, and without her even knowing it her arms went out to him, and in a second he had crossed the rest of the space to her and she was in his arms, strained against his chest, her head buried against his shoulder.

'Oh Michael,' she said, 'people have been saying such awful things about you ever since you came here, and everyone seems to want to arm me against you and warn me off, as if you were some kind of white-slaver, or drug-peddler, or something.'

'Oh, but I'm worse, far worse,' he said, and she felt him laughing. 'I'm like the marauding. Dane who plunders the town and snatches away the womenfolk. I can understand them of course. Any town that had a jewel like you would naturally be jealous of any stranger taking it away. They're jealous, that's all. Take no notice of them. Here, here, don't cry, don't cry Anne darling – not on my best suit.'

'Oh don't!' she laughed in the midst of a sob.

'There, you don't know if you're laughing or crying. Here, sit down with me, that's right, dry your eyes. I've got another present for you. In my pocket. Stop crying and I'll give it to you.'

He was like a man with a child, but then she'd been behaving pretty much like a child. She dried her eyes and blew her nose, sitting on the sofa with his arm round her, a strong arm, and the one she wanted to be there. Then, when he judged she had stopped sniffing, he dug his had into his pocket for the present. She was reminded of that terrible moment when Joe had put his hand in his pocket and brought out the unwanted engagement ring.

'There,' he said. 'Some lovely expensive Swiss chocolate. You can't buy it in Winton, so that proves I've been away.'

She took it and laughed shakily. 'I thought you weren't going to offer me proof,' she said. Although it only proved he'd been away, not when.

'That was when you wanted proof. But you don't want it now, do you? You've made your mind up without it.'

'Yes,' she said. 'I suppose I have.'

'I learned a long time ago, Anne,' he said, suddenly serious, 'that there's no use in arguing against suspicion. It only makes it more suspicious. If someone accuses you of something they think is wrong, they'll make up their minds whether you're guilty or not without any help from you. Anything you say only adds fuel to the fire.'

That expression of disappointment that had crossed his face – had she reminded him then of that other person who had failed him in this way?

'Who was it who taught you?' she asked shyly. He gave her a hug and looked down into her face with affection.

'I'll tell you some time. Not now.' Then he smiled and attempted to lighten the atmosphere.

'You can't expect me to give away all my secrets in one go.'

'No. I can wait,' she said. 'Would you like a cup of tea? I can put the kettle on while I put these in water.'

'I thought you'd never ask,' he said. 'I think your other flowers need removing, poor things.'

The bluebells Joe had brought her. Typical of him, as the roses were typical of Michael. But the bluebells were dead now, wizened into brown ghosts in the vase. She picked up the vase and took it with her to the kitchen, thinking as she did so that he did not ask her who had brought her those flowers. He didn't ask those sorts of question – he was stronger than she. When she came back with the roses arranged in the vase she thanked him for them again and kissed him; she had forgotten the bluebells and had almost forgotten the quarrel.

When Dad came across from the station they were sitting on the sofa reading the paper together and talking in low, relaxed voices. They made a pretty picture, sitting there with their heads together in complete harmony, and had Dad not had his heart set on Joe, he might have taken courage from the sight and worried less about his only daughter being left on the shelf. As it was he only said,

Oh, you've got a visitor. I'll make myself scarce.'

'Don't be silly, Dad, Anne said, jumping up and kissing him on the cheek. 'You sit down and I'll make another cup of tea for us all. Do you want a sandwich as well?'

'Hm. Could do with one, I suppose.'

'All right. You sit and talk to Michael. I won't be long.'

She said that, but she was as long as she could reasonably be, to give them the best chance of getting into conversation, and when she came back with the tray she found that, as she had expected, Michael's charm had worked on Dad and he was telling the younger man all about rabbits and the glorious days of steam, his two greatest passions.

It was quite late when Michael eventually took his departure, promising to pick Anne up on Saturday night and take her to the dance at the Villiers Hotel in Winton Magna. Anne went with him to the front door to see him out and to get another breathtaking kiss.

'Well at least I've convinced your father I'm not a white-slaver,' Michael said when he finally released her.

'Oh, Dad's all right. He's just a bit suspicious of strangers.'

'*Strangers*! How long before I stop being considered a stranger?'

'In Winton it generally takes about forty years.'

'Thank heaven I don't have to wait that long. I wasn't talking about Winton, foolish,' he said, giving her a final kiss. 'I was talking about you.'

Twelve

The dance at the Villiers Hotel was held every year, and was a large and well-attended affair, and Anne was privately glad that Michael had returned in time to take here there. She was also, even more secretly, glad that Fate had arranged it so that she went with Michael rather than with Joe, for she had already discovered that Michael was as competent a dancer as he was everything else, whereas Joe could only do the walk-round to slow music, known locally as 'the smooch'. When he had taken her to dances, they seemed to spend most of their time standing around in groups chatting, while Anne watched the whirling dancers with distant envy.

All in all, she decided, the occasion called for a new dress, and having dispatched such household chores as her father allowed her to do, she got out her bike and cycled into Market Winton. The town was always full on a Saturday, with a different kind of crowd from Thursdays. Now it was women out for their big shop of the week, with pushchairs and sweet-sucking kids, while Dad carried the smallest on his back and sometimes held the lead of a straining mongrel dog. It was odd how all the townspeople's dogs were ill-trained like that, and whatever speed their owners were walking, they would pull so hard against the lead that they would progress on two feet only and make an unearthly gargling noise as the collar choked them.

There was also a lot of local young lads, roaring aimlessly up and down the narrow High Street on motorbikes, or leaning in groups against their push-bikes on the car park behind Woolworths. The young girls went about in pairs, looking in the dress shops, standing outside the record-mart listening to the latest tunes, and pretending not to notice when the youths called out to them. The old folk toiled very slowly up the side streets looking for bargains, or laboured even more slowly up the stairs to the coffee bar on the first floor of Hiblett's for a cup of milky coffee and a rock-cake and their weekly natter to their fellow-pensioners.

Anne loved it all, of course, and made the most of her slow cycle through the town. She always felt that there were three Wintons – the ordinary weekday one, the Thursday one, and the Saturday one. It compensated a little for living in the same place for so long, and such a small place at that. Her destination that morning was the cobbled street known as Gobs Alley, which led off the High Street and was lined with shops which, by chance or design, had all been turned into clothes shops, shoe shops, record shops, and similar places of interest to young people. It had once tried to style itself the Carnaby Street of Winton. It said in the local guide book that the name was originally God's Alley, because it had led up to the long-defunct monastery; Anne remembered from her school days a ruder explanation the boys had thought up.

There was in Gobs Alley, however, a very good little boutique which Anne had patronised before, and having chained her bike to one of the bollards at the foot of the street she walked towards it. She hadn't gone more than a few yards, however, when Wendy came out of the record shop at the bottom and joined her with a cheerful greeting.

'Hello! Are you better? Of course you are, or you wouldn't be here. Going to the dance tonight?'

'Yes,' said Anne. 'Are you?' She was rather cool, not knowing quite how to take Wendy after that business about the restaurant.

'But of course. That's why I'm here – to buy a new dress, something that will shake Winton to its Roman foundations and write my name in the town's history. What are you doing here?'

'I've come to buy a new dress too,' Anne admitted. Wendy nodded happily.

'Good, then we'll look together, and you can tell me if things suit me or not, and I'll do the same for you.' And she tucked her arm through Anne's as they walked on. 'Who are you going with tonight?' she asked next.

'Michael,' Anne said, watching her sideways for a reaction. Wendy did not seem at all surprised. She merely nodded with polite interest. 'Who are you going with?'

'I'm not sure,' Wendy said. 'I'm going there with Roberto, but I have a kind of feeling I agreed to meet Graham there, so there might be an almighty blow up. I wish I could remember. I'd ask him only he's been on his week's holiday, and he doesn't get back until this afternoon.

Oh well, I suppose it doesn't matter too much. Shall we go in here?'

'I was intending to,' Anne said as they reached her favourite shop. They went in and sifted through the rack of dresses, hovered over by a minute fourteen-year-old with a habitual sniff who helped out on Saturdays. Wendy gathered up three or four things and hared off to the changing room, and Anne went on sifting more slowly until she found what she was looking for. It was flame-red chiffon with drooping sleeves, and a skirt in two layers, with jagged ends, like the party dresses of the nineteen-thirties. It was her size, too, and she followed Wendy with it happily.

When she tried it on, it was just right, as she had known it would be. The vivid colour set off the darkness of her hair and the clear pallor of her skin, and the style, of course, was exactly hers. Wearing it still and taking sideways glances at her reflection, she waited for Wendy to decide on what she wanted. It was one of those communal changing rooms, so she could stand and talk while Wendy tried on one thing after another.

'I have a fancy for black,' Wendy was saying. 'The Italians think it's sexy.'

'But Roberto isn't Italian,' Anne pointed out. 'He's only an Italian waiter.'

'I know, I know. Must you spoil my illusions?' Wendy said, straining at the zip of a black crêpe sheath.

'Didn't you try to spoil mine?' Anne said. Having said it, she found she was shaking.

'Did I?' Wendy said vaguely. 'Do the zip up for me, will you? I can't shift it.'

'You've got it caught in the material. Stand still! Yes, you did, you told me Michael was in Roberto's restaurant with another woman last week.'

'Oh, was he? Naughty old Michael. There now, what do you think? Not too hot, eh?'

'Not hot at all. The point was, he wasn't there.'

'Who wasn't where? Undo it again, will you?'

'Michael wasn't at the restaurant.'

'That's good,' Wendy said even more vaguely from the depths of the dress. 'I think I like this one better anyway. Give me a hand.'

'Well, why did you say he was there if he wasn't?' Anne asked, feeling she was getting nowhere.

'I don't know. I must have thought I saw him if I said so, mustn't I?'

'But he says he wasn't there.'

'Then there's nothing to worry about is there?' Wendy said reasonably. 'I don't think black suits me after all.'

'I could have told you that in the beginning,' Anne said gloomily.

'Why didn't you, then?'

'I didn't want to spoil your illusions,' Anne countered, and Wendy stuck her tongue out at her friend's reflection.

The red dress continued to look just right. Anne was glad, for sometimes a purchase loses some of its glamour when you get it home, but this looked, if anything, even better, when she finally put it on with her silver sandals and her string of pearls, having spent nearly a hour over her face and hair. Happiness added its own glow to her looks, and when Michael arrived (in plenty of time and an Aston Martin!) he looked at her for some seconds before saying anything.

'Well, do I look all right?' Anne asked at length.

'I can't think of anything to say that would be adequate,' he said, taking her hands and looking at her in a way that made her tingle. 'You're beautiful.' And he kissed her, carefully so as not to rumple her. 'Shall we go? I thought we could have one drink on the way so as not to arrive too early. Would that suit you?'

'Anything you say,' Anne said equably. 'Is that *another* car I see?'

'Oh yes, it's one I brought back from Birmingham with me. I have to tune it and deliver it back, so I thought I'd get a ride out of it while I have it. Lovely cars.'

'It looks sporty,' Anne agreed. 'I must say goodbye to Dad, and then I'll be ready.'

They were not the only people to stop off for a drink at The Bull, the nearest pub to the Villiers. There were several other couples in the doubles bar there, all dressed for the dance, and among them was Wendy with a saturnine youth who looked at least three years younger than his partner.

'That must be Roberto, the Italian waiter,' Anne said to Michael. She was glad she had someone as mature-looking as Michael to brave the crowds with. Wendy however was match for anyone, and she came bouncing over as soon as she saw

Anne, and the dark boy followed her. He was wearing a very tight velvet suit, which might account for his preoccupied air. It looked as though it might split with any unexpected movement.

'Hello, there you are!' Wendy greeted them. 'Hello, Michael. Do you know Roberto? Roberto, this is Anne and Michael.'

'How do you do,' Anne said politely.

''ello,' Roberto said. Anne wondered if that was 'Hello' in Italian, or if he had adenoids.

'You bought the blue one in the end,' she remarked to Wendy, who still hadn't chosen a dress when Anne had left her in town that morning.

'You'll never guess who I've just seen,' Wendy broke in, without noticing the remark.

'Whom?' said Anne and Michael together, and they turned to grin at each other.

'Old Joe Halderthay with a lady on his arm – didn't we, Roberto? And guess who the lady was?'

'Who?' they chorused again.

'It was the new lady vet from Upwood. How about that for sensational news? He certainly works fast; she hasn't been there for more than a week or so. And she's quite reasonable looking.'

'Why shouldn't she be?' Anne said, nettled at what she thought was a slight on Joe. She felt Michael looking at her with a raised eyebrow, and she pressed his arm to reassure him.

'Oh well, you know what vets are like – they're usually bunchy women in old tweeds and felt hats. But this one's quite young and pretty. Well, at least, she isn't ugly.'

181

'Let's have a drink, shall we?' Michael said, feeling that enough had been said on this particular subject. 'What does everyone want?

'No, let me,' Roberto said. It was adenoids, Anne decided.

'Thanks, old chap,' Michael agreed graciously. 'Just a tonic water for me – I'm driving, and I don't want to use up my allowance too soon. Anne?'

'Gin and tonic please, with lots of ice.'

'My usual, please,' Wendy said, and Roberto nodded and departed. 'I've taken to drinking Campari-soda,' she said when he had gone' 'so don't stand too close to me or I'll clash with your dress. Such an uncompromising colour, red. You have to be a real beauty, like Anne, to wear it. I'd look like a plate of mashed swede if I tried it on.'

The drinks, when they came, seemed to loosen Roberto's tongue, and he turned out to be good fun in a quiet way. Wendy was at her irrelevant, amusing best, and the four of them enjoyed themselves so much that when it was time to leave they stayed together and drove up to the Villiers in Michael's car.

The dance was filling up quite nicely. They handed in their tickets in the ante-room, and went to drop their wraps and powder their noses while the men waited and did whatever men do while women powder their noses.

'He's as gorgeous as ever,' Wendy said to Anne as they shared a mirror.

'Who, Roberto?' Anne asked, surprised.

'No, Mr Martini. You're a lucky girl.'

'Am I?' Anne mused. She looked at her smiling reflection. 'I suppose I am.'

The large ballroom was softly lit and decorated with flowers, and already a couple of dozen couples were dancing to the excellent band. The bar was crowded, as it always, mysteriously, is at dances, and there was a separate buffet room where the food was being laid out for later in the evening. They spent some time walking around and saying hello to the various people they knew, and Anne noticed how most people stared at Michael, some with envy and some with suspicion. She kept her hand on his arm, and once he squeezed it and said,

'You see how they all look on me as a stranger.'

But when she glanced up at him, he was laughing, so it was all right. They didn't meet Joe and his lady yet, though Wendy said she saw him across the other side of the room. However, Anne was now inclined to give less credence to what Wendy saw at any kind of distance.

The doctor was there with his wife, a pleasant, grey-haired lady with a limp, whose interest in dances was, therefore, more social than athletic.

'Hello, Anne – you look ravishing,' he said.

'So you do, Anne,' said Mrs Ross. 'Won't you introduce us to your partner?'

Anne did so, and the doctor and Michael shook hands, and Michael bent over the doctor's wife's hand in a graceful way that made her smile.

'Did your father have a look at that house?' Dr Ross asked.

'We both did,' Anne said. 'I could tell he loved it on sight – as I did, really, only I think it

183

probably will be too small. I should think it's only got one room downstairs and two tiny ones up, and we might get on each others' nerves in such a small space.'

'Leave home then,' Dr Ross suggested at once. 'I don't know what a great girl like you is doing anyway, living under her father's wing. It's well past time you spread your wings and flew away.'

'George, you shouldn't bully people,' his wife remonstrated gently.

'People need to be bullied. They like it, anyway,' Dr Ross affirmed. 'You go out and see the world, young Anne, while you *are* young. Time enough to settle down in dear old Winton when you get creaky with age, like me. Not like you, Marjorie darling, I hasten to add!' And his wife smiled. 'Why don't you marry her, young man,' the doctor went on incorrigibly, 'and take her round the world. That would solve her father's problem. He could move into that little cottage and be settled for life.'

'If I marry her, sir,' Michael said with a suppressed smile, 'it won't be for her father's sake.'

Anne looked up at him with wide eyes, and he winked without moving the rest of his face. The doctor's wife saw it, and tugged at her husband's arm.

'Come away George, you embarrass the young people. Goodbye for now, Anne, and give my love to your father.'

'Not the world's most tactful man,' Anne said softly as they moved away.

'He's all right,' Michael said musingly. 'Shall

we dance? After all, it's supposed to be what we came for.'

'I'm ready,' Anne said.

They danced for about an hour, enjoying the movement and the conversation. They passed Wendy once or twice, her eyes tightly shut like someone on a big dipper, being whirled in a Come Dancing manner by her dark friend, who seemed to be managing to do very nearly everything in his tight suit without splitting it. Wendy opened her eyes when Anne called to her, and then shut them again.

'I can't look!' she called back as they twirled past. 'I don't think he's even got a licence. Can you be fined drunk in charge of a woman?'

When the band stopped for their break, Anne and Michael were luckily placed quite near the door, and managed to get into the bar before the big rush, but the people were pressing in so tightly that they were glad to get their drinks and get out.

'It's very hot – can we go outside for a minute?' Anne said.

'Are you sure you should?' Michael asked. 'You might catch cold again, after being so hot.'

'I'll be all right,' Anne said, surprised that he should show such concern. 'I'll tell you at once if I feel chilly.'

'See you do,' he said, and they carried their drinks out onto the veranda overlooking the hotel's garden.

'Phew, that's better. Mm, doesn't the night smell gorgeous!'

'It does,' Michael agreed gravely. 'What is it?'

'Oh a bit of this and a bit of that. Night-scented-stock, and wet grass and trees, and wistaria. Just mainly the night.'

'And it's so quiet. I can hardly get used to the quiet out here, after the city.'

They stopped talking and just listened to the blissful hush of the night away from the ball-room, and they remained in silence, sipping their drinks, for some time, feeling companionable without the need to talk. Michael slipped his arm round Anne's shoulders to check she wasn't cold, and left it there, drawing her in a little closer to him. When they had both finished their drinks, they put their glasses down on the parapet, and then Michael put both arms around her and kissed her, and for a time they became just another of the shadowy couples making their own world on that moonlit veranda.

'Happy, darling?' Michael asked at last.

'Mm,' Anne said, smiling up at him, which was enough.

'Not cold?'

'No, but I'd like to have another dance.'

'Let's have one more drink first, and then we'll go in. Will you have the same again?'

'Yes, all right. I'll wait here for you. I don't want to push into that crowded bar.'

'I didn't intend you to, my little flower,' Michael grinned. 'Don't get talking to any strange men while I'm away.'

As if he had forseen what happened next, no sooner had Michael disappeared through one set of doors, than Joe appeared through another. He paused, looking up and down the veranda, and

Anne froze, hoping he would not see her. But Joe's eyes were good. His head lifted slightly as he spotted her and hunted around for her companion, and then, after a slight hesitation, he came towards her.

'Hello, Joe,' Anne greeted him resignedly. 'Having a good time?'

'Are you alone?' he asked her, ignoring the question.

'Temporarily. Are you? Where did you leave your partner?'

'My—? Oh, you mean Miss Brown?'

'I don't suppose you call her Miss Brown all evening to her face, do you?'

'She wanted to come, and she had no one to come with. I've had these tickets for ages, so I didn't see why I should waste them,' Joe said, anxious to explain. Anne made a flat gesture with her hand.

'Joe, you don't need to tell me. It isn't my business. You're entitled to come to the dance with anyone you please. I was just wondering what she'd think if she knew you'd deserted her to seek me out.'

'It isn't like that,' Joe hastened to explain, his face reddening a little.

'I don't care what it's like,' Anne said, beginning to feel a little impatient at his desire to involve her with his personal affairs.

'No, but I wanted you to understand, because, well, I wanted you to realise why I'm worried about you.'

'You've no need to be worried,' Anne said evenly, and a wiser man, or perhaps one less infatuated, would have taken warning, but Joe blundered on.

'Oh but I am, when I see you still with that man. I don't want you to be hurt, Anne, and believe me—'

'I don't want to hear it,' Anne said sharply, turning away. Joe was so wrought up that he actually caught hold of her arm, and held it in quite a tight grip.

'Anne, you don't know what he's like.'

'Don't I?'

'You don't know the things he's done. He's—'

'I don't want to hear you!' Anne shouted, and several heads turned. She lowered her voice, but said with no less intensity. 'I don't want to hear your opinion of Michael. I don't want to hear anything you've got to say about him. Is that clear?'

'Anne, I have to tell you.' His grip had tightened without his knowing it, and his fingers were biting into her arm. 'He's been seeing another woman in secret all the time. I've seen him with her.'

'You're hurting me. Go away. Let me go and go away!'

'Yes, go away, why don't you?' Michael's voice came from behind Joe. Anne caught his glance across Joe's shoulder. He was carrying two glasses, but even as he spoke he put them down carefully and came another step closer. Joe did not release her arm, but he turned to face Michael, glaring at him angrily.

'You keep out of this!' he said. 'It's none of your business.'

'It is my business,' Michael said coolly. 'I'm making it my business. Let go of her.'

'You've no rights here,' Joe said. 'It's not for you to tell me to go. If Anne wants me to go away it's for her to say.'

'Well she's said so, hasn't she? And you haven't gone. So now I'm saying it – beat it pig-man.'

Anne felt Joe jar at the insult, as if at a blow. He let go of her arm abruptly and straightened up. 'Don't you call me that!' he said furiously. 'Who the hell do you think you are?'

Anne stared from one of them to the other. Joe was not so tall as Michael, but he was broader and heavier, and looked the more dangerous of the two. His big hands were balled into fists, and the muscle bulged inside his ill-fitting jacket. Michael, dark and slim, looked more like a dancer. Anne saw quite clearly, with the insight of love, that he was afraid of the heavier man, but was too proud to show it. He stood erect and poised, forcing himself not to flinch, and to smile coolly. The atmosphere was almost tangible between them, and she half expected them to emit sparks of anger.

Joe made the beginning of the move that would undo Michael, and at that moment Anne threw herself between them, and folded her own two hands round Joe's fist even as it was raised. He shook her off, but by old habit could not do it roughly, and she caught his hand again more strongly and tried to prise open the fingers.

'Stop it, Joe! Please stop it,' she said, looking up at him pleadingly while he still glared unmoved over her head at his antagonist. 'Please give it up and go away. Stop it, do you hear me!'

She shook the fist she held, and at last he dropped his eyes to her and looked at her first angrily and then, as the anger faded and the love took its place, with a puzzled expression.

'Anne, you don't . . . really . . . you don't love him, do you?'

Now it was Anne's turn to become aware of the implications of the scene. She looked up at Joe, Joe whose face was as familiar to her as her own, and knew that Michael was standing behind her, listening. She didn't want this to be happening. She didn't want to have to say the words that would break Joe's heart, and perhaps make her more vulnerable than she had ever cared to be. But it had to be the truth, now. She gulped, and said,

'Yes, Joe.'

'A man like him?' Joe asked, his brow furrowed. 'You can't mean it.'

'I do.'

'A man you have to protect? A man who can't even stand up for himself?'

'Joe, his way isn't yours. There's more than one kind of courage. You've no right to accuse him. You don't understand.'

'No, I don't,' Joe said bitterly, and now he withdrew his hand sharply from her grip. 'I don't understand.' He turned away from her so that she couldn't see his face, and his voice was muffled as he said, 'I'm sorry, Anne. I hope everything will be all right for you. I hope he's good to you.' And then he was gone, striding

190

away down the veranda with his head high against the curious, and perhaps mocking, stares of the onlookers.

Anne and Michael watched him go. Anne held herself rigid against the emotions inside her, and waited in apprehension for Michael to break the silence. If he said something cruel or mocking, it would tear her. But after a moment he moved to her and touched her hand lightly and said in a very gentle voice,

'Poor bloke. He really loved you.'

Anne let him take her hand for the comfort. 'Yes.'

'And you chose me instead of him. That must have been a blow to his pride.'

'Don't let's talk about it,' Anne said. 'Let's go inside and dance. I want to forget it.'

'As you like,' Michael said, and, slender and dark and elegant, without Joe's good looks as Joe was without his charm, he escorted her back into the ballroom through the same avenue of curious stares that Joe had had to negotiate a few moments before.

'Poor bloke,' Michael murmured again. 'At least I got the girl.'

Yes, she thought, you got the girl: but how absolutely she was his captive she was only just beginning to realise. She wondered if he knew the depth of her commitment. So much she loved him, that she would forgive him even the dark-haired woman – even that dark secret.

For the other woman was fact – she knew as she knew the sun would rise tomorrow that Joe would not lie about that to her. He had been

seeing another woman. Perhaps it was an inno-
cent relationship. Perhaps he had a good reason
for keeping it a secret from her. Perhaps he was
not even lying about not meeting her in the
restaurant, and Wendy was mistaken after all.

But whatever the truth was, Anne knew that
she had to accept the situation, she had to trust
him. Belief comes from the inside, he had said:
and inside her, her living self knew that he was
for her. Wordlessly, senselessly, her heart believed
in him. He had woken the sleeping tiger, and
she knew that if he wanted her, she would go
with him to the ends of the earth, for that was
the adventure she had waited for all her life.

Thirteen

'The fight I never had seems to have established me as a Winton character,' Michael said, breaking off a grass stem and putting it in his mouth. They were sitting on top of a cliff overlooking the sea. There was no one else in sight, not even a building or a boat, and they could see for twenty miles around.

'Don't suck that,' she warned him. 'You'll get enteritis.'

'Too late,' he said, taking the end out and staring at it. 'I've already sucked it. Besides, if I'm going to become a local character, I'll have to start chewing straws.'

'I'll ignore the intended slight on my fellow yokels,' Anne said, lying back on the short mossy turf and squinting up at him. 'Anyway, what do you mean about the fight?' .

'Only that people keep coming up to me and telling me bits of local news. I'm sure they wouldn't have done if I hadn't stood up to your ex-boyfriend in a public place.'

'Don't mock,' Anne said, but without heat. 'What have they told you then. And who's they, anyway?'

'I've been told,' he said solemnly, rolling over on one elbow and gazing down at Anne from directly above, 'that the young lady vet from Upwood has got engaged. And that she's not wasting any time – she's put the banns up, too.'

'You're kidding!' she exclaimed. Michael bent down to kiss her and she pushed him away, eager for news. 'No, don't, tell me properly about this.'

'What ever happened to romance?' he sighed. 'Am I always to play second fiddle to a pig-man?'

'You mean it's Joe? Tell me!'

'Yes, she's getting married to your Joe. Are you happy about that?' he asked her curiously.

'Not my Joe any more,' she said automatically. 'Yes, of course I'm happy about it. I'm sure they'll be very happy together. Reading Marx and raising pigs.'

'That comes very close to being catty,' Michael warned her.

'It wasn't meant to be. He's buying that piece of land, you know, to start up on his own.'

Michael nodded. 'I got told that too. But of course you knew it first.'

'Could hardly help it seeing we're his family solicitor. Hers too, now. But I'd never have made a farmer's wife. I should have realised that long ago. Continually battling with the rising price of feed and the falling price of meat. The diseases and the vet's bills – though I suppose he won't have any of those if he's marrying one – and the sows that die in farrow and the piglets that get overlaid. And the work, day after day after day. No leisure time for a farmer, *or* his wife. No going away for a fortnight in Benidorm. Just the farm, for ever.'

She shuddered. He laughed at her.

'What a scene of horror! And to think you only just escaped it!'

'Only just,' she agreed gravely, looking up at his dear, lopsided face and his far-seeing eyes. 'Saved from a fate worse than death.'

'And what do you intend to do with your life, now you've been reprieved?'

'That depends.'

'On what?'

She could hardly say, on you. Why didn't the world arrange itself so that a woman could propose as well as a man, instead of remaining in this state of anticipation week after week?

'On lots of things. My father, for instance. I'd like to see him settled in that little cottage he's fallen in love with, but for him to do that, I'd have to leave home.'

'That sounds dramatic. But it's not a big step, you know. Lots of people leave home every day and survive the experience.'

'It's a big step the first time you do it. And to set off for an unknown destination alone—'

'Oh, you're thinking of going alone, are you?'

'Well, who do you think I should go with?'

'Whom.'

'All right, then, whom?'

'It depends where you're thinking of going,' Michael countered, and seeing her frustrated expression he laughed again and rolled over onto his back to look at the sea again. 'Seriously, though, I've been wondering if you'd like a change of scene.'

Anne's heart was beating a little faster, but she concealed it, and spoke calmly.

'Such as?'

'Well, you've been working for that same firm for such a long time. How about a new job? How about coming to work for me in the new showroom?'

'As what?' Her calm voice was not an act now.

'Receptionist and saleswoman. There's nothing men like better when they're buying a car than to have it shown off to them by a pretty girl. And the fact that you're well known here would add to the authenticity of the bargain. They'd trust a car you showed them.'

'What about the female customers?'

'Well, I'd deal with them, of course.'

'Of course,' Anne said, a small smile tugging the corners of her lips. 'But it wouldn't solve Dad's problem.'

'I'd thought of that, too. You could have the flat above the garage. It's small – hardly more than a bedsitter really – but it would be a start towards independence.'

'And where would you be living, if I had the flat above the garage?'

'The flat above the showroom of course,' Michael said. Anne smiled faintly at him, and then shook her head.

'It wouldn't do.'

'Why wouldn't it?' he asked, although he half knew what she was going to say.

'Because the two flats share the same staircase. People would talk.'

'You mean people would think I was visiting you at night,' he said flatly. She nodded. 'But

196

my dear girl, I could visit you at night wherever you were living.'

'People don't see it that way. Besides—' she hesitated. 'It would look – so *particular.* It would look as though we were going to get married.'

'What do you care what people think?' he asked her, with a peculiarly wry expression.

'I do care,' she insisted.

'For other people's opinion of you? Does it matter?'

'Yes, it does,' she said stubbornly. 'Not strangers, it isn't their business. But when you live in a small place like Winton, you can't do anything without it getting back to people you know and love – people like Dad, and the doctor, and people you care about and who care about you. And it hurts them, *because* they care about you.'

'No man is an island?' Michael suggested.

'Yes, if you like,' Anne said. 'At any rate, nothing you do affects only yourself. If you think that, you're selfish and blind.' Then, realising she had been laying down the law rather firmly, she added lamely, 'At least that's what I think.'

'So the upshot is,' Michael said, not looking at her, 'that you wouldn't live in the flat above the garage unless we were going to be married?'

'Not until after you've gone,' she said, trying to bring a touch of lightness into the conversation.

'Gone?'

'Well, you won't be staying in Winton for ever, will you? You'll be moving on after a year or two, won't you?'

'Will I?'

'I don't know. Don't keep answering my questions with questions. I thought you were the roving type, who never settles down.'

'I always intended to settle down eventually, when I found the right place to be and the right person to be with,' he said. He picked another grass blade and put it to his mouth, and then remembered, and with a sideways glance at her threw it down again. 'I always wanted to think I'd have a home eventually. It's a sad thing to be rootless.'

'Well, if you want to settle in a small town, you'd better put ideas like living in the same house as a girl out of your head.'

'Unless I marry her?'

'Unless you marry her.'

'And you wouldn't live in the same house with me unless we were married?'

'I've said so.'

'And you wouldn't take the job and the flat I've offered you unless I married you?'

'You're getting there, chum.'

'And that's the only reason you'd marry me?'

'Wait a minute, who's talking about marriage?'

'I thought we were.'

'Not as far as I remember. You offered me a job, that's all I remember being offered.'

Michael looked at her sideways again, and then grinned ruefully. 'I lost my nerve at the last minute,' he said.

'I don't believe you!'

'I did. I was going to ask you, and then I lost my nerve. I kept hoping you'd ask me, and save me the trouble.'

'How could I ask you?' Anne said astonished. 'Really!'

'Oh, I suppose not. It's very hard you know, having to say these things.'

'What things? And how would you know it's hard? Have you tried before?'

Michael jumped up and went onto his knees beside her, taking both her hands and putting on a moonstruck face which did not conceal the genuine emotion in his eyes.

'Darling Anne, will you marry me?' She did not answer at once, and he went on, 'I have to warn you that I might not be all I've been cracked up to be. I might settle down and become an ordinary unexceptional husband with a mortgage, and stay in the same town for years on end. Could you bear that?'

'I wanted excitement, and adventure,' Anne said.

'I might contrive to provide you with a bit of the first, though adventure makes its own rules. Unless you can tell yourself that all of life is an adventure. That always seemed to me a very handy philosophy for the nine-to-fiver with a mortgage and a pram to push.'

'I should think it might be an adventure marrying someone I knew absolutely nothing about,' she said. 'Nothing but his name – and no proof even that it *is* his name.'

'Do you think I'd make up something like Frederick?' he protested.

'For an alias it *is* a bit unimaginative,' she agreed.

'Then you'll do it? You'll marry me?'

'How could I refuse when you ask me so

nicely?' He clutched her hands, grinning like an idiot, and then kissed them fervently.

'Good girl!' he said laughing. 'We'll have such fun! Everything we do will be fun!'

'Even paying bills?'

'Who's going to pay bills? We've got a car. When there get to be too many of them, we just drive away to another town.'

'For goodness sake! Don't say anything like that in front of Dad. He'd have fourteen fits. He might just believe you.'

'Who said I was kidding?' he said with a straight face.

I have to believe you're not, she said, but only to herself. She knew nothing about him, nothing at all. It was possibly a grave mistake she was making. But she'd have made as bad a mistake marrying Joe, whom she knew inside out. It might not be everyone's way, but it was hers, and she had to live by her own nature.

'We'd better go back and tell Dad,' she said. 'He'll be able to have his cottage, and keep rabbits after all. But we'll stay in Winton for a month or two, won't we? To let him get used to the idea. He'd worry so if we went away altogether, just at first.'

'Yes, we'll stay, until he stops thinking of me as a stranger,' Michael said, taking her hand to help her up. She stood up in one movement, and was wrapped around by his loving arms and kissed for her effort.

'I wouldn't promise that, if I were you,' she said, 'or I'll never get to see the world.'